Kim Lawrence

THE ITALIAN'S SECRETARY BRIDE

EXPECTING!

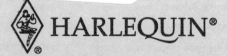

HARLEQUIN®

TORONTO • NEW YORK • LONDON
AMSTERDAM • PARIS • SYDNEY • HAMBURG
STOCKHOLM • ATHENS • TOKYO • MILAN • MADRID
PRAGUE • WARSAW • BUDAPEST • AUCKLAND

ISBN-13: 978-0-373-12780-1
ISBN-10:   0-373-12780-4

THE ITALIAN'S SECRETARY BRIDE

First North American Publication 2008.

Previously published in the U.K. under the title
LUCA'S SECRETARY BRIDE

Copyright © 2004 by Kim Lawrence.

HARLEQUIN®
Presents

Welcome to the December 2008 collection of
Harlequin Presents!

This month, be sure to read Lynne Graham's
The Greek Tycoon's Disobedient Bride, the first
book in her exciting new trilogy, VIRGIN BRIDES,
ARROGANT HUSBANDS. Plus, don't miss the second
installment of Sandra Marton's THE SHEIKH TYCOONS
series, *The Sheikh's Rebellious Mistress.* Get whisked
off into a world of glamour, luxury and passion in
Abby Green's *The Mediterranean Billionaire's
Blackmail Bargain,* in which innocent Alicia finds
herself falling for hard-hearted Dante. Italian tycoon
Luca O'Hagan will stop at nothing to make Alice his
bride in Kim Lawrence's *The Italian's Secretary Bride,*
and in Helen Brooks's *Ruthless Tycoon, Innocent
Wife,* virgin Marianne Carr will do anything to save
her home, and ruthless Rafe Steed is on hand to help
her. Things begin to heat up at the office for interior
designer Merrow in Trish Wylie's *His Mistress,
His Terms,* when playboy Alex sets out to break
all the rules. Independent Cally will have one night
she'll never forget with bad-boy billionaire Blake in
Natalie Anderson's *Bought: One Night, One Marriage.*
And find out if Allie can thaw French doctor
Remy de Brizat's heart in Sara Craven's
Bride of Desire. Happy reading!

We'd love to hear what you think about Presents.
E-mail us at Presents@hmb.co.uk or join in the
discussions at www.iheartpresents.com and
www.sensationalromance.blogspot.com, where you'll
also find more information about books and authors!

EXPECTING!

She's sexy,
successful…
and
PREGNANT!

Relax and enjoy our fabulous series about couples whose passion ends in pregnancies… sometimes unexpected! Of course, the birth of a baby is always a joyful event, and we can guarantee that our characters will become wonderful moms and dads. But what happens in those nine months before?

Share the surprises, emotions, drama and suspense as our parents-to-be come to terms with the prospect of bringing a new baby into the world. All will discover that the business of making babies brings with it the most special love of all.…

Delivered only by Harlequin Presents®

All about the author...
Kim Lawrence

Though lacking much authentic Welsh blood, **KIM LAWRENCE**—from English/Irish stock—was born and brought up in north Wales. She returned there when she married, and her sons were both born on Anglesey, an island off the coast. Though not isolated, Anglesey is a little off the beaten track, but lively Dublin, which Kim loves, is only a short ferry ride away.

Today they live on the farm her husband was brought up on. Welsh is the first language of many people in this area and Kim's husband and sons are bilingual. She is having a lot of fun, and developing a few headaches, trying to learn the language!

With small children, the unsocial hours of nursing weren't too attractive, so, encouraged by a husband who thinks she can do anything she sets her mind to, Kim tried her hand at writing. Always a keen Harlequin reader, it seemed natural for her to write a romance novel. Now she can't imagine doing anything else.

She is an avid gardener and cook, and enjoys running—often on the beach, because, as she lives on an island, the sea is never very far away. She is usually accompanied by her Jack Russell, Sprout—don't ask, it's a long story!

CHAPTER ONE

THE grateful mother had hysterics: the very loud, attention-grabbing variety. She certainly grabbed the attention of the shoppers, tourists and locals going about their business in the busy New York thoroughfare on the sunny late afternoon. A large crowd was gathering to hear her express her tearful gratitude to the man who had saved her baby's life.

The 'baby' in question added truculently that he was *not* a baby, he was nearly five, before kicking the man who had snatched him from the jaws of death on the shin.

Luca's fixed smile grew strained as he hung onto the kid who, even after his brush with death, had not made the connection between danger and moving traffic. As the screaming monster tried to bite him Luca found himself wondering just what the attraction of parenthood was. From where he was standing it wasn't exactly glaringly obvious.

Luca liked children as much as the next man, and of course it went without saying that any child of his would *not* try to bite people, but he felt no primal urge to get out there and procreate. Not that this was an issue as yet. Despite his reputation for being a bit of a maverick, Luca actually held some pretty traditional views, and in his book marriage and children came as a joint package. Though as he had never to this point in his life met a woman he would contemplate spending the rest of his life with, it was kind of academic.

Being of mixed Italian and Irish parentage, Luca had never been left with any doubt that one of his primary duties in life was to find a nice wife and produce babies...*no pressure*! That he had reached thirty without doing either did not go down well with his parents or, for that matter, his grandparents, aunts and uncles and cousins.

Luca's response whenever his single status was mentioned was to point out he had an elder brother who could carry on the family name. Clearly this subject came under the heading of the duty of the first-born, and what was Roman—thirty-two?

Luca himself would be more than happy to fulfil the role of doting uncle, something that would not require too many sacrifices, compromises or sleepless nights on his part. Unfortunately there were no likely candidates that he knew of on the scene to marry his brother right now.

Unless, he mused with a cynical grimace, you included the ever-present and incredibly faithful Alice, who would no doubt marry her boss like a shot if she ever got within sniffing distance of a ring.

Luca moved his head in an almost imperceptible negative gesture as an image of grey-blue eyes and pale silvery blonde curls appeared in his head.

The hardness that filtered into his eyes as he considered the question of his brother's indispensable blonde right-hand woman apparently communicated itself with the child he was restraining. Flashing the tall man a wary look, he ran back to his mother.

'I hate you!' the boy yelled from behind the protection of her skirt.

'I'm not wild about you either,' Luca responded absently. His thoughts were momentarily elsewhere.

His brother wouldn't actually consider marrying his blonde secretary, would he? He didn't love her, but as it seemed his brother had grown cynical in his old age and given up on love that might not be the obstacle it might once have been.

Just *how* jaundiced and disillusioned his brother had become had been revealed in a recent conversation. The occasion had been their parents' anniversary and their father had not wasted the opportunity of a captive audience to introduce his favourite theme.

Later that night they had been walking beside a lake on the extensive family estate in Ireland.

'Subtle, wasn't he?' Luca remarked ironically to his brother.

'As ever, but he might have a point, you know.' Roman, his expression unreadable, paused to skim a stone on the lake's still surface. 'It's all in the wrist,' he explained modestly.

'You don't say.' Luca punched the air in exaggerated triumph as his own stone outskipped that of his brother. The mocking enactment of the sibling rivalry that had once existed between them drew a smile from his brother. 'You're losing it, Roman,' he taunted before pressing curiously, 'Have you been holding out on me? Is there someone I don't know about?'

'Someone…?'

Luca spelt it out. 'Have you fallen in love? Will the parents disapprove of her? *That* would be interesting. God, she's not married, is she?' That would *really* put the cat amongst the pigeons, he thought.

'You think love is a good enough reason to get married?'

'I've not given it a lot of thought. I take it *you* don't.'

'Love is a form of temporary insanity,' his sibling informed him. 'Insanity is not a good basis for any contract I can think of, and when you get right down to it that's what marriage is…a contract.'

Luca didn't consider himself a particularly romantic man but he found this assessment of the institution of marriage chilling. 'Not a meeting of souls?'

'You need a soul mate to be complete? Do me a favour!'

'I feel pretty complete,' Luca agreed. 'But, can you imagine Da without Ma or vice versa?'

'There are exceptions,' Roman conceded grudgingly. 'I tried

doing the love and marriage thing.' The stone Roman flung sunk. 'In case it slipped your mind, things didn't go according to plan.'

Luca restricted his show of fraternal sympathy to a bang on the shoulder. 'You're not going to let a little thing like being dumped at the altar turn you into a lonely, bitter bachelor?'

'Oh, I'll get married, but *love* will not be high on my list of requirements. In fact it won't be on it at all,' Roman revealed with a cynical grimace of distaste. 'Marry now...marry in five years—what's the difference?'

What if this hadn't been an example of his brother's warped black sense of humour? What if he was on the lookout for a mother for his children? What if he wanted *Alice Trevelyan*?

Now wouldn't that be a joke? Joke or not, it didn't make Luca smile. Now the crazy idea had occurred to him Luca found it was one he didn't particularly warm to. It was patently obvious to him that Alice Trevelyan was *not* the wife for his brother.

There was any number of sound reasons to back up his conclusion—at least he was sure there would be had he chosen to work them out. Sometimes it was better to go on gut instincts and on this subject his guts were *very* definite.

The frown between his darkly defined brows deepened. There was propinquity to be considered, you couldn't underestimate the power of that, especially when the item you were constantly in close proximity to came attached to curves of a very superior quality.

The fact that his brother's secretary was easily the sexiest-looking woman Luca had ever come across had to be an influencing factor. She didn't flaunt it in revealing tops and short skirts, nothing clung, but somehow she managed to look more provocative in pearls and sensible shoes than another woman would have done naked.

Roman's Alice was the sort of female most men would not be satisfied to simply look at...she was the sort who made a man want to touch. His sculpted mouth tightened into a grimace filled with self-mockery; he could personally testify to this. Not that he would go anywhere near a woman of his brother's even if watching her walk across a room could send his imagination into overdrive.

No way was he going to jeopardise his relationship with his brother to satisfy a fairly basic itch.

But he was assuming Roman wanted Alice. He never had figured out exactly what his brother's relationship with his secretary was. They certainly had a rapport in the office, Luca had seen it for himself, but did that rapport extend as far as the bedroom…?

He hadn't asked and he wasn't about to. If his brother chose to mix business with pleasure—a recipe for disaster in his book—that was Roman's business.

'Deserve a medal, pal…' Someone slapped him hard on the shoulder. Luca said something appropriately self-deprecatory. He didn't want a medal; he wanted out of there before someone produced a camera.

Damn…the crowd was starting to attract a bigger crowd.

Attention was the last thing Luca wanted. He spent what sometimes seemed to be an inordinate amount of energy avoiding attention, although, it had to be admitted, not always successfully.

He could see the headlines now…something to do with his old journalistic instincts? It was almost ten years since he had worked on the national broadsheet where he had cut his teeth straight from school, but he still possessed an insider's knowledge of how a journo's mind worked. Being able to occasionally anticipate the pack sometimes came in very handy.

Ironic, really, that if it hadn't been for his father's heart attack he might still be part of that pack. When Finn O'Hagan had been forced into early retirement it had been Roman, who had the financial expertise, who had stepped in to run the highly successful leisure and property side of the family-run outfit.

Before his heart attack Finn had been planning to offload

the unprofitable Stateside publishing firm inherited from an uncle. It had only been sentiment that had made him continue to subsidise the loss-making operation this long. Luca had agreed to take a short sabbatical, step in, go through the books and generally put the place in good enough order to put on the market. He'd cleared his calendar for a couple of months.

Then something strange had happened. Luca had started enjoying himself and his enthusiasm had been contagious.

By the end of the first year they had been out of the red, had signed up a prolific new author who had not been out of the best-seller lists since his first week of publication and had attracted several established names. No longer the poor relation in the O'Hagan empire, they now had offices in Sydney, London and Dublin and Luca was still enjoying himself.

Luca gently but firmly detached the weeping woman from his shirt-front and scanned the gathering crowd as he smoothed the expensive fabric back into place. The action made him aware that he hadn't escaped unscathed from the incident. A slight frown formed on his lean, handsome face as he flexed his right shoulder experimentally and felt the burn of over-stretched muscles.

Had some of the interested observers been privy to his private resolve to find time in his schedule to take more exercise, they would have been startled; Luca possessed a streamlined, long-legged muscular body—broad of shoulder, narrow of hip—that would have earned him a fortune advertising male swimwear.

The arrival of a man Luca assumed to be the kiddy's father was the cue for lots more tears. Greeted with the garbled explanation that his son and heir had escaped death by the narrowest of margins, the poor guy went into shock.

Luca decided to take advantage of the moment to slip away.

Melting into a crowd did not come easily for Luca. Being six four in his bare feet and the owner of a body that had come in the top three of a celebratory magazine poll of 'the man you would most like to see naked,' it was fair to say he stood out in a crowd.

He knew about the article because some joker in his Dublin office had pinned said article on the bulletin board along with the readers' letters in the next issue that contended the vote must have been fixed, and indignantly suggested that Luca had been robbed of first place.

Despite his natural handicaps he did manage to make a successful escape. Once he was out of sight and earshot of the crowd his phone rang. It was his brother, his single brother. Luca smiled in grim amusement when he realised that for a couple of minutes back there he'd almost had Roman locked into a loveless marriage.

Talk about letting your imagination run away from you.

Would it have run quite so far, and so fast, if the bride he had saying *I do* hadn't been Alice Trevelyan? He frowned as the unwelcome thought surfaced in his mind, and pushed it away.

'Are we still on for tonight?'

Luca glanced at his watch and grimaced. 'Sure thing, only I've still got to catch up with Hennessey. I could be a few minutes late.'

'And will the lovely Ingrid be with you?'

'Funny guy,' Luca said with a grin in response to the innocent enquiry.

'Tenacious lady, isn't she, and if ever there was a born self-publicist?'

'You put her onto me, didn't you?'

'*Me!* I'm heartbroken…my confidence is shot to hell, what man wouldn't be? Dumped for my own brother.'

'*Dio mio!* You're a devious snake is what you are,' Luca retorted.

'Give me a break, Luca. I had to do something, the woman kept planting stories about spring weddings. And it came to me…it's well documented that Luca likes blondes, especially tall Nordic ones. So I mentioned in passing that *you* get invited to all the A-list parties, and I let it drop that you're much more photogenic than me and infinitely more high profile, especially in the States.'

Luca couldn't help appreciating his brother's tactics. 'You knew she was gay, of course.'

A chuckle reverberated down the line. 'Did she sound you out on donating sperm at some future date too?'

'Yes,' Luca gritted with a shudder. 'Although she made it clear that would depend on me passing stringent medical screening.'

'And I thought I was special…' His brother sighed soulfully. 'About tonight, no problem, Alice and I are running late too. See you lat…by the way, I probably should warn you it's possible that Alice believes the tabloid version of you and Ingrid.'

Luca could hear the grin in his brother's voice. 'And you saw no reason to straighten her out?'

'Strangely enough that didn't occur to me. She thinks I'm being quite extraordinarily brave,' he confided.

'You're warped, you know that.'

'She thinks you're a heartless love rat,' Roman explained, not bothering to hide his amusement.

So no change there. 'Will Alice be there tonight, then?' he asked casually.

'Of course she will. Alice is almost family.'

Almost…? Luca slid the phone back into his pocket, a thoughtful expression on his face… *Am I being paranoid?*

Don't lose sight of the fact that, even if asked, Alice might say no to Roman, Luca told himself.

Sure, that's *really* going to happen. We are talking the woman who without a second thought took a knife wielded by a raving lunatic to save her boss, he reminded himself.

So look at this another way. Would having Alice Trevelyan as his new sister really be so bad?

A spasm of distaste crossed his face. *Yes, it definitely would!* Well, if I can't find another bride for Roman, I might just have to marry the woman myself!

'Can I get you an aperitif?' the solicitous waiter asked.

Alice wasn't normally a drinker, but she felt that under the circumstances a little Dutch courage might not be such a bad idea.

All I had to say was no. Why was that so hard? She comforted herself slightly as she sipped slowly on her glass of white wine with the recognition that she wasn't the only person who found it hard to say no to her boss. Her employer had the enviable knack of getting people to do what he wanted.

Slow or not, in an hour and a half you could sip quite a lot, and there wasn't much else to do *but* sip as she sat conspicuously alone amongst the other people, or rather *couples*, dining in the exclusive New York hotel. It was at times like this a girl could be excused for thinking she were the only person left who wasn't part of a pair. She felt a flicker of pain as she reached unconsciously for the gold ring that she had worn on a chain around her neck since the day her worried mother had confided she was afraid her daughter wasn't letting go of the past.

You're young, Alice, and you know as well as I do that Mark would want you to get on with your life.

Discovering its absence made her feel more undressed than the low-cut dress that had forced her to remove it tonight.

With a pang Alice turned her head as the couple seated to her left touched fingers across the table. Not being a girl to dwell on the gloomy aspects of life, she reminded herself of the many benefits of not having a significant other.

If she had a lover she would have to worry about the hedgehog style her hair adopted when she woke up in the morning. She could sleep on whatever side of the bed she wanted—and right now the bed she occupied was a rather spectacular queen-size.

Roman was many things, she mused, but a stingy employer

was not one of them. When she travelled with him it was always first class. She occupied a gorgeous room right next to his on the top floor.

Alice looked at her empty glass and hazily considered the possibility that she had had too much to drink. But didn't people who were drunk feel happy and carefree, prone to dancing on tables and breaking into song at the least provocation?

Alice felt no inclination to do either.

She had no illusions about it. At best the evening was going to be an endurance test of her self-control. The thought of spending a painful hour, or even *two*, trying to make polite conversation with someone who had enough ego in his little finger to sustain a small planet was something she was not looking forward to.

And when it came to filling the inevitable awkward silences she knew better than to look to her dining companion for help. He'd just sit there looking bored in that aggravatingly languid way he had with those eerily penetrating blue eyes of his giving the unnerving impression he could read her thoughts.

The irony of the situation didn't escape her. An intimate dinner with a single man who was universally acknowledged as being not only wealthy and smart but also unbelievably good-looking would have had most women turning cartwheels and here was she acting as if Judgement Day had arrived.

Of course most women, unlike Alice, didn't know what a pain in the rear Luca O'Hagan actually was. Given the choice between root-canal work and dining by candlelight with her boss's younger brother, Alice would have headed for the dentist's chair every time.

The problem was he was spoilt. Things came too easily to the man, she decided, staring broodingly into her empty glass, including female company, she thought disapprovingly. Perhaps, she mused, he might have been more tolerable if someone had actually ever said *no* to him. Having seen him in action personally, she wasn't holding her breath! The title 'babe magnet' had never been more aptly bestowed.

Her soft but determined chin rose to a decisive angle. She'd give him ten more minutes and then she was going to go back to her room to order a sandwich. Feeling a lot better for having made the decision, she caught a waiter's eye and ordered another drink.

At the same moment the voice of the *maître d'* drifted across the room. 'Your favourite table…'

Alice's fingers tightened around the stem of her glass and her slender back stiffened. Having worked for her millionaire boss for the past five years, she immediately recognised the warm 'very special person' welcoming tone.

What was it about some people that made other people fall over themselves to be attentive? Alice would have liked to be able to attribute the deference to money and power, but she knew that even if you had robbed her boss and his brother of those advantages they would still have been able to effortlessly command attention in any environment.

Impatient with the trepidation she was experiencing, she turned her head and gave a smile befitting the efficient 'PA cum secretary deputising for her boss's face.

There was a man standing there, but not the one she was waiting for. Anticlimax sent the tense muscles of her stomach into a lurching dive. She sighed, rubbed her nervously damp palms against one another and, because she'd looked at most everything else in the room and the newcomer was worth a second glance, she carried on studying him.

This one looked far more like the sort of man she would *prefer* to be waiting for, she mused wistfully. Tall but not *too* tall and well dressed. Youngish-looking, too, despite his distinctive head of silver hair. As her eyes connected with his the man gave a quizzical smile. Alice returned a lopsided embarrassed smile and looked away in case he got the wrong idea.

Her gloom intensified as she returned her attention to the wine list and pretended to study it, as if she couldn't already have written a dissertation on the hideously expensive bottles on offer! The man, like the entire room, including the overly solicitous staff, obviously thought she had been stood up. They weren't wrong.

Just as well this wasn't a real date.

The idea of her having a real date with Luca O'Hagan made her smile thinly. World peace by the weekend was a much more likely scenario!

She was making inroads into her fresh glass of wine when the discreet *maître d'* quietly informed her that Mr O'Hagan had left a message that he would be there presently.

'I can hardly wait.' Her dry rejoinder made the bearer of the glad tidings look slightly disconcerted. 'Thank you,' she added with a smile, trying hard to display a little of the gratitude the man obviously expected her to exhibit.

In reality the news had not made Alice feel exceptionally grateful, just exceptionally mad.

To be stood up by, not one, but *two* O'Hagans on one evening was enough to make anyone a little cranky.

'You stay, smooth things over with Luca for me,' her boss had cajoled persuasively before abandoning her. 'A night out will do you good. You deserve a treat.'

'Well, actually, I could do with an early night…' And you could do with therapy if you imagine even for a tiny second that I'd class a night out with your brother as a treat.

'Pity. I cancelled our meeting last month and I wouldn't like Luca to think I'm a sore loser.'

Alice was instantly sympathetic. 'Well, I suppose I could…'

'Excellent.'

What Roman had lost and Luca had picked up had been six feet one and blonde. The Swedish model in question graced the front covers of just about every glossy magazine Alice picked up at the moment. The elder O'Hagan brother had returned from a business trip to Prague to find that his girlfriend had left for the States with his brother.

Roman hadn't seem gutted; he had greeted the news with a philosophical shrug. Alice, indignant on his behalf, knew he was bravely hiding his true feelings. Bad enough to have your brother run off with your girlfriend, but for the story then to be splashed across the tabloids must have been truly shocking.

She really hoped her boss's feelings for the gorgeous lady hadn't run deep, but even if they hadn't it wouldn't have let the lecherous Luca off the hook in her eyes. For all he knew Roman might have been head over heels in love…no, Alice thought, he had behaved despicably!

Some things *nice* people didn't do, and pinching your brother's girl was one of them.

But then nobody had ever called Luca nice. Instead, they'd called him other things, including sinfully sexy!

While there was no denying he had something special in the looks department, Alice's personal taste ran to something far less in your face and obvious.

Her eyes wandered across the room to the quiet alcove the newcomer had been escorted to and found that coincidentally he was looking her way. She nodded slightly in acknowledgement and looked away. Maybe he'd been stood up too? Although he didn't look like the sort of man that would happen to.

God, why did I let Roman talk me into this? Maybe Luca was right, maybe I am *Roman's doormat*. Even now, a long time after overhearing the contemptuous remark Luca had made, it still had the power to make her blood boil.

The notion that she was some sort of slave without a mind or will of her own was totally unfair. Luca's assessment of her relationship with her boss had been so far off the mark to be laughable.

For some reason Luca O'Hagan couldn't stand her and he didn't make any effort to hide the fact. The tight feeling in her chest got tighter as she contemplated the sneers and snubs, besides the despised 'doormat' jibe, she had been on the receiving end of courtesy of Luca O'Hagan. What had she ever done to him except bleed a bit on the upholstery of his car? Hardly a crime to justify a vendetta.

Her method of dealing with his sneers and him was polite indifference. You couldn't really start a slanging match with the brother of your boss, especially when he ran part of the family company. So Alice maintained a supernaturally serene front in face of his frequently provocative behaviour, a fact of which she was extremely proud. Fortunately their paths didn't cross too frequently as he spent most of his time this side of the Atlantic and her time was split between Dublin and London.

'Excuse me…?'

The Texan drawl startled Alice from her own thoughts. Her eyes widened when she lifted her head and saw the silver-haired new arrival standing at her elbow.

'I'm dining alone and I was wondering…?'

Alice, aware that his remark could be heard by fellow diners, felt her face flush. 'I'm waiting for someone.'

There was no question of her encouraging him, but the attention of an attractive man did make her feel a little less like a total loser sitting amongst the romantically inclined couples surrounding her.

He gave a rueful grimace. 'I never thought otherwise…but until then, would you like some company? I promise you I'm perfectly harmless.' His smile was as charming as the line was clichéd.

This claim wrenched an unwilling laugh from Alice. 'That I doubt. Actually I was just leaving.'

'You've been stood up?'

'It looks like it.'

'The man must be crazy.'

'No, just incredibly self-centred, insufferably rude and deeply obnoxious.'

CHAPTER TWO

EVEN without turning her head Alice could pinpoint the exact moment Luca O'Hagan walked into the place from the ten-second hush that descended on the candlelit room, followed by an interested low-voiced buzz of speculative comment.

She could visualise him in her mind's eye. He would act as if he didn't know his tall, imposing figure was the focus of attention as he wove his way with innate grace between the tightly packed tables, but he was. He knew *exactly* what effect he had on people and wasn't, she thought contemptuously, above exploiting it cynically when it suited him.

She smiled and tried to give the amusing tale the silver-haired Seth was relating the attention it and he deserved; it wasn't easy when she knew who was approaching. Seth paused expectantly and she laughed at the punchline...at least I hope it was the punchline, she thought.

An invisible presence and Luca was still a disastrously distracting person. Only if you let him be, she told herself sternly. There was no question of her own reaction to Luca being anything out of the ordinary; he was the sort of man who drew a reaction from people. Love or hate the man—she identified with the latter group—nobody ignored him!

Personally, the attraction of being the partner of a man who stopped conversations and drew covetous stares from other women when he walked into a room passed her by. Not a problem you're likely to have, the dry voice in her head pointed out cruelly.

She dragged her attention back to the man sitting opposite. He was telling her about an art exhibition he had attended the previous month. Actually he seemed one of the few people unaware of the buzz in the room that accompanied the tall man who came to stand by his shoulder.

'What have you done with Roman, then?'

There was no trace of the charm he was famed for in the terse, deep-pitched accusing enquiry. And you expected there to be, Alice? she asked herself. He reserved his *niceness* for people who mattered and clearly she didn't.

Alice didn't look up, but felt the familiar prickle of antagonism slide down her spine as her nostrils flared in response to the subtle male fragrance he sparingly used.

Experience had taught her that the first few moments of making contact with Luca O'Hagan were generally the worst; practically speaking this meant she kept eye contact to the minimum and didn't say the first or even *second* thing that came to mind. If she managed not to trip over her own feet or say anything too stupid in those first few seconds she could generally pass for someone who could bear to be in the same room as him without wanting to crawl out of her own skin.

'He's not here.' And I wish I weren't, she thought, picking up her glass to avoid focusing on him.

'That much I can see for myself.' There was the sound of a chair scraping the floor as he pulled one out from the table and sat down.

'He got called away…it was urgent.' There was an expectant silence, until belatedly she remembered her manners. 'This is Seth…Seth…erm?' She turned to her companion with an apologetic grimace. 'I'm terrible with names.' Before her entertaining companion could refresh her memory Luca spoke up.

'Chase,' Luca supplied. He nodded casually towards the older man. 'How are you, Seth?'

In Alice's eyes it counted in the Texan's favour that he didn't appear even slightly bothered by the perceptible coldness in Luca's manner. She was definitely inclined to think well of someone who wasn't blighted by Luca O'Hagan's disapproval. In her opinion there were far too many people—many of whom ought to know better—already willing to stand on their heads if it made him look at them warmly.

'Pretty good, thanks, Luca.'

She slid a sideways covert peek at Luca's classical profile; it looked like granite only not as warm. Her eyebrows twitched as she looked away. My, someone has got out of bed the wrong side today, she thought.

Whose bed? Was the model still his 'constant companion', as one of the gossip columnists had triumphantly revealed the previous week? she wondered sourly. Or had the woman seen the light?

She brought her speculation to an abrupt halt. Pathetic people with no life of their own got more excited by the love lives of celebrities than their own, she reminded herself severely.

Of course, I know this celebrity and I don't actually *have* a love life to speak of. But the principle is the same. It is pathetic.

Nobody watching as she looked from one man to the other would have guessed at how her stomach was churning. It had become a matter of pride with her *not* to react to Luca's volatile moods; the fact her stately calm irritated him was a plus point.

'You know one another?' she asked, trawling frantically through her memory to recall how she had described Luca to Seth. What she remembered made her cringe. The *one time* I speak my mind and get smart—now what were the odds on that? She just hoped that Seth would keep the joke to himself.

Luca's eyes skimmed her face; he looked faintly impatient. 'Obviously.'

'I met Luca a few years back when I was over in Ireland buying horses from his mother,' Seth explained. 'My dad wanted to introduce some new breeding stock.'

A glimmer of humour flashed in Luca's eyes as he said, deadpan, 'My father was saying something similar to Roman and me only the other day.'

'He takes an interest in the stud?'

'Since Dad retired he has a lot of time on his hands. He uses it to *take an interest* in all sorts of things,' Luca returned smoothly.

'Likes to keep his finger on the pulse still, does he?' Seth sounded sympathetic.

'He's not quite got the hang of retirement yet,' Luca admitted. 'If it wasn't for Ma I think he'd still be behind his desk. How long have you and old Seth here,' he asked Alice, 'known one another?'

'About ten minutes,' she replied without thinking.

His dark-winged sable brows lifted in expressive unison. *'Amazing...'*

'Why amazing?' she queried suspiciously. Did he think she was lying? It required considerable self-discipline to smile serenely.

'I got the impression you were *old friends.'*

Not a liar, just a tart, she mentally corrected. Oh, that's all right, then. It was important on occasions like this to keep your sense of humour.

'What is this—an interrogation?' she wondered lightly.

More to the point, why am I feeling guilty? she asked herself angrily.

'Perhaps we were close in another life,' the American, who had been silent during their spiky war of words, spoke up.

His frivolity earned him a repressive frown from Alice before she turned her attention back to Luca. 'Seth took pity on me.'

'Pity wasn't my main motivating factor.'

'That,' Luca responded drily, 'I can well believe.'

Alice, her voice raised, interrupted this little male byplay. 'And if he hadn't I'd already be in my room ordering room service.'

Her pointed comment was wasted on Luca, who responded

with an amused if cynical sneer. 'That's Seth all over—a
regular Sir Galahad,' he drawled.

Her bosom swelled with indignation as she fought to control
her temper. 'Something nobody is likely to accuse you of
being.'

She saw the startled expression flash across Luca's face and
felt a surge of reckless satisfaction.

Luca set his elbows on the table and said in a deceptively
indolent drawl, 'I've read that inappropriate sarcasm often
masks anger.'

This from the man who specialised in the cutting one-liner!
She was an amateur compared with him; Luca's savage wit was
as ruthless as a surgeon's scalpel.

'I'm sure you know much more about inappropriate sarcasm
than I do.' Try guessing what this smile is masking, she thought,
delivering a smile of brilliant insincerity.

'She's got you there, Luca.' Seth laughed. 'You know, before
you arrived we were just—'

'Sure…whatever…' Actually it had been pretty obvious
what they were *just*… The dull thud in Luca's temple cranked
up another painful notch as he recalled the scene that had met
him as he'd arrived.

He hadn't needed the directions given him to locate his
table. He had heard her laughter the moment he had walked into
the room, soft but huskily intimate.

He wasn't the only male whose attention was drawn to the sexy,
inviting sound either. Half the men in the room were annoying
their partners by risking a sly look. No doubt if the opportunity
had arisen to do more than look they'd have jumped at it!

And you wouldn't? Being an essentially honest man, he
couldn't dismiss the possibility he'd be tempted…all right,
more than tempted. Especially in that dress, he thought as his
eyes slid over the clinging fabric that revealed the full swell of
her deliciously rounded breasts. His body reacted to her, so
what? That just made him male and alive. That his basic—*very*

basic—first impulse had been to throttle the life out of the man who was leering at Alice was not so easily explained away.

Roman might be prepared to accept a loveless marriage of mutual convenience, but no way would he accept a wife who when his back was turned flirted with any man who happened along. Luca doubted he and his brother were *that* different!

Alice was furious on Seth's behalf. Luca could not have made his boredom more apparent if he had yawned.

'How is the lovely Natalia?'

'She's fine. I think Seth thought that flirting with her would lower the price. He discovered it didn't; my mother,' he confided, 'takes no prisoners when it comes to business.'

'A family trait,' Alice muttered under her breath. The way Luca had turned the ailing publishing house into a dynamic, thriving business was an achievement that had earned him international respect. She knew for a fact that any number of well-known firms who had suffered financial setbacks had offered him indecent sums of money to work his magic for them.

'I flirted with your mother for pleasure, not profit,' Seth protested. 'She is a very beautiful woman.'

'Beauty runs in the family too, or so I've been told.'

I just bet you have, Alice thought.

'Damn, I thought I'd switched that off.' Seth grimaced and pulled a trilling phone from his pocket. 'Could you excuse me for a minute, folks?' he said.

'What runs in *your* family, other than blonde hair?' It took Alice, who was watching Seth's retreating back with dismay, a couple of seconds to realise that Luca had directed the question to her.

She pretended to consider his question before replying mildly. 'I think I'd have to say a dislike of people who can't look you in the face when they talk to you. You know the type I mean—shifty…sly…no manners…'

Luca, whose blue eyes had been unashamedly trained on her

cleavage when he had mentioned her hair, and still were, gave a lopsided grin. He gave a shrug that acknowledged her hit and lifted his head.

Their eyes clashed.

The satisfyingly superior feeling, the product of having won a bout in this war of wits, evaporated about the same moment that her stomach muscles tensed with excitement. *Excitement…?*

'I thought you'd have been insulted if I hadn't noticed.'

If there had been even a hint of embarrassment, a trace of apology, in his attitude she might have forgiven him. Alice sucked in an angry breath. *Brazen!* she decided wrathfully. There was no other word to describe him…unless it was charismatic, beautiful and sexy.

'Insulting me has never bothered you before.'

'I didn't think you'd noticed.'

Unbelievable…did he think she didn't have feelings? 'I noticed.' Her lashes came down as it struck her forcibly that there was very little about Luca that she hadn't noticed. She frowned at this growing evidence of her unhealthy fascination.

Without turning his head, Luca halted the approaching waiter with a soft, 'no, we're not ready to order.'

Her spine stiffened with a snap and the jolt made her head spin—or was it the lack of food, or possibly that last drink? Her generous lips tightened into a disapproving and indignant line as she focused on the handsome face of her reluctant dining companion.

'*I* was ready to order two hours ago,' she informed him tartly.

One slanted sable brow rose as he scanned her flushed face and overbright sparkling eyes. 'I was unavoidably detained.'

'What was her name?'

Obviously she regretted this unwise comment the moment it had left her lips. She was uncomfortably aware that it was the sort of critical complaint a jealous girlfriend competing for his favours would have come out with.

Something she wasn't.

Actually Alice doubted that any girlfriend of Luca O'Hagan's who did complain, or demand to know where he had been and with whom, would retain that honour for very long. There would always be someone to replace her; Luca believed firmly in the theory of safety in numbers!

Alice decided to tack on an addition that would establish her disinterest in the subject of his love life, but instead heard with a deepening sense of dismay, *'Or didn't you ask?'* fall waspishly from her lips.

Oh, God...! She removed her stare from his darkly handsome face and made a detailed study of the bottom of her glass.

A short static pause followed her sarcastic jab.

'Actually I—'

'Spare me the details!' she cut in, her stomach muscles shifting nauseously at the prospect of him filling in the blanks in her imagination. *Still* she couldn't stop her runaway tongue. 'I suppose some men just never grow up.'

Luca looked at her with a worrying lack of expression. 'Am I to assume that you number me amongst these cases of arrested development?' A muscle in his lean brown cheek visibly clenched as their glances locked. 'Why is it you never lose an opportunity to look down that little nose of yours at me...?' He paused, a bemused frown drawing his brow into creases. Then unexpectedly he reached out to lightly graze the tip of the feature under discussion with his knuckle.

Alice, who literally jumped back in her seat, was too startled by the physical contact to register that the action had all the hallmarks of compulsion about it. She couldn't register much beyond the deafening thud of her heartbeat echoing dully in her ears.

Luca's sensually sculpted lips thinned into a cynical smile as his hand fell away.

'Why did you do that?' she asked.

'Damned if I know.' Not strictly true. He'd always wanted to touch her, to feel for himself if that alabaster-clear skin was actually as sensationally smooth as it looked; would his fingers glide over the silky surface?

Alice, who had been expecting some smart sarcastic response, found she couldn't meet his eyes. The direction of the conversation was seriously spooking her, as was the tension that weighed heavily in the air.

The uncomfortable silence seethed with things she didn't care to analyse until finally she could bear it no longer. 'Oh, and there's no need to apologise for being late. I've really had a lovely time sitting here for nearly two hours.' Angry, very blue eyes lifted from the depths of her glass and behind the anger lurked an awareness that she was blowing her years of super-natural serenity well and truly out of the water.

'I'm very sorry I'm late.'

She gave an unimpressed sniff. 'No, you're not.'

'*Per amor di Dio!* I think this is what you'd call a no-win situation.'

'It wasn't spontaneous…'

The scraping sound as Luca shifted his chair to give himself some extra leg-room made her jump nervously. Holding her eyes, he slowly crossed one ankle over the other.

'When I *spontaneously* admired your dress you didn't like it.' A slow, dangerous smile spread across his lean face. 'Or maybe you did?' Her angry gasp made his smile widen.

'It wasn't my dress you were looking at!' she countered huskily.

Luca's cerulean-blue eyes drifted downwards…

Alice bit her lip and endured the scrutiny even though she felt like crawling out of her skin. She lifted her chin up, angry stare fixed straight ahead; no amount of will-power could prevent the rosy wash of warm tell-tale colour inexorably rise up her neck.

Grow-up, Alice, she told herself angrily, it's not as if he's actually *looking*. He's just trying to wind you up. This is probably his idea of a joke. That resentful theory fell apart when his glance lifted. There was nothing that faintly resembled humour in his expression.

'You're right, I wasn't,' he agreed sardonically.

Alice met his eyes and her breath snagged in her too-dry throat before she looked away again, deeply shaken by the predatory gleam in his fantastic eyes.

She pressed her hands against her thighs and took a deep restorative breath. Under the table her knees carried on shaking uncontrollably. If she had stood up at that moment she would have fallen flat on her face.

She knew that her reaction was way, *way* over the top. For starters she wasn't his type at all…heck, the man was probably *born* looking predatory. Far from finding her attractive, he probably wouldn't notice if she were sitting there stark naked.

A militant light sparked to life in her eyes. It wasn't that she wanted Luca to notice she was a woman, it was just the acknowledgement that she couldn't have made him notice even if she had wanted to that hurt her self-esteem.

My God, but there was no justice in the world, she thought, her temper uncharacteristically flaring. She hadn't actually expected the latest diet fad to turn her into a flat-chested clothes-horse, but after three weeks of self-deprivation it would have been nice to have lost a pound!

Not that anyone would have noticed, she thought with a self-pitying sniff.

'Anyway, we're not talking about my clothes sense, we're talking about your total lack of consideration.'

'*We* are? You should have said. Right, I'm *extremely* sorry I'm late.'

Luca's electric-blue eyes might not be what you expected of a Latin male, but everything else about him was—including his volatile temperament, off-the-scale insolence, and in-your-face sex appeal. It was pathetic really that he traded on his sexuality. Her deliberate attempt to view his tall, athletically lean six feet plus frame with amused condescension did not prevent the fluttery sensation in the pit of her stomach.

She cleared her throat; even so her voice held a husky rasp as she bowed her head slightly in grudging acknowledgement. 'Apology accepted.'

The pout was something he had not seen before, Luca registered, removing his eyes from the heaving contours of her generous breasts, which he *had* been conscious of on other occasions.

Several occasions, actually.

Even when she was in the less-revealing sexily discreet silk blouses she habitually wore during working hours a male's eyes were inevitably drawn to the full, feminine contours—even his, and Luca considered himself a pretty controlled sort of guy. If he weren't he would have told his brother the screamingly obvious fact that it was always a bad idea to have a personal relationship with someone who worked for you.

The line between Alice's feathery brows deepened as Luca leaned back in his chair with indolent grace. Her eyes were drawn to his hands as he laid them on the table; his long, tapering fingers were brown and shapely.

'Very gracious of you. Tell me, so that I know next time…do you always make the rules up as you go along?' he asked.

'At least I know that rules exist.' If ever a man had been born to push the constraints of society to the limit, it was Luca. He was a born risk-taker. As she turned her head to avoid contact with his compelling eyes she caught sight of something that made her eyes widen. 'Have you been fighting?'

Luca tilted his head and ran a hand lightly along the hard curve of his jaw. Almost imperceptibly he winced. 'You should see the other guy.'

Earlier in the subdued light Alice had missed the discoloured area extending from one sharp-edged cheekbone to his chiselled jaw. Now that she looked she could see there were also signs of faint puffiness in the skin around his sculpted lips.

'You think this is funny?' She didn't bother to hide her disapproval of his attitude. Violence was a subject upon which she held strong views.

In her opinion, no matter what the situation, an intelligent person—and there was no denying that Luca, for all his faults, had a mind like a steel trap—could *always* come up with a better solution than physical violence.

She was not even aware that her hand had come to rest on her midriff. The doctors had done a pretty neat job, but she would always bear the permanent reminder of the day that she had been the victim of an act of violence—the first day, coincidentally, that she had ever laid eyes on her employer's younger brother.

Memory triggered, she recalled the night he had carried her in his arms. Now it seemed like something that had happened to someone else...actually it always had. Her memories of the occasion were hazy, restricted to Luca cursing fluently in musical Italian when all she'd done was ask how Roman was. That and a series of impressions left in her head...warmth, lean hardness, strength, the male scent of his skin overlaid lightly with the subtle fragrance he had been wearing.

Perhaps it had been the relief, the instinctive knowledge at some deep level that here had been someone who would shoulder the burden of responsibility. She'd been able to let go, she hadn't had to be in control and strong. Maybe that was why these details remained so clear in her mind.

His prompt action had saved her life, they had said. Even if this statement had been a little over-the-top she would undoubtedly have been in trouble if he hadn't been there.

Though you could hardly compare the trauma of the two incidents, they were intrinsically linked in her mind. The day she had got in the way of a stalker's knife, not even her own stalker, and the day she'd first seen Luca O'Hagan.

'Have you seen a doctor?'

Luca, his eyes trained unblinkingly on her face, didn't

respond to the querulous abrupt enquiry. Their eyes connected and she knew that in that uncomfortable way Luca had he knew exactly where her thoughts had been. Belatedly aware of the hand pressed to her middle, she let it fall self-consciously away.

His mouth softened slightly as he studied her downcast features. 'It was a minor accident, that's all, Alice.' Actually he had got the bruise from saving the child earlier.

Her gaze lifted. It wasn't very often he used her name, but when he did she always felt an odd insidious weakness work its way through her body. She worked very hard not to let him see that it was happening right now. 'Roman got called away.'

'So you said.'

'I did...?' she echoed vaguely.

'I suppose Roman standing you up explains the mood.'

'The mood? I don't have a mood.' Her frown deepened. 'Why,' she demanded, 'are you looking at me like that?'

'How many of those have you had?' His eyes touched the glass in her hand.

'Not nearly enough,' she told him sincerely.

His lips twitched. 'When was the last time you ate?'

Alice released a long, shuddering sigh as her eyes followed a splendid creamy confection topped by a lattice of calorific spun sugar being delivered to a nearby table. 'Three weeks ago,' she confessed.

Luca blinked. *'Three weeks ago...?'*

Alice nodded. 'Real food. I've been on a diet.' In her book powdered stuff that tasted of nothing when you mixed it with milk and as many grapefruit as you could stomach did not constitute food in the real sense of the word. 'Crazy, isn't it? Half the world are starving and the other half are trying to slim.'

'Diet? What on earth are you dieting for?'

Alice delivered a look of killing contempt. Only someone who wasn't carrying an ounce of surplus flesh on his hard-muscled frame could say something so spectacularly stupid.

'I'd have thought that was abundantly obvious,' she gritted. 'Especially,' she added gloomily, 'in this dress.'

She was viewing the despised curves of her body when it occurred to her that her comment had virtually invited his scrutiny. She closed her eyes tight as horror washed over her. *Why do I keep mentioning this darned dress?*

She hardly dared look up, but when she gathered the courage she discovered that he had not refused her invitation! She tried to act as if it didn't bother her that his eyes were superglued to her body, but by the time he got back to her face her breath had increased to a degree she couldn't disguise. From where he was looking he must have been aware of the fact.

'It's *abundantly* obvious in that dress that most women would kill for the figure you've got. You have a body that would feature in nine out of ten men's fantasies,' he pronounced.

Alice gave a nervous laugh. '*Sure!*' she said.

'You don't think I'm serious?' He seemed perplexed by her attitude.

'People do not design clothes for women my shape.'

'That's because people wouldn't be looking at the clothes,' he immediately rebutted.

'Then what would they…?' She stopped and blushed darkly.

Luca grinned. 'Exactly,' he confirmed, looking amused by her embarrassment. 'Now, how about if we order?'

'I'm not hungry and, besides, it would be rude to order before Seth gets back.'

'You'll eat anyway, if only to soak up the drinks you've had, and Seth doesn't need to come back on my account.'

'Are you suggesting I'm drunk?' Alice demanded, indignant at the slur.

His lips curved in a sardonic smile. 'Aren't you?'

'Not saying what you want me to doesn't make me drunk.'

'I think when you review this conversation tomorrow morning you might want to revise that opinion.'

'Are you saying I'm talking rubbish?'

'You're talking. Normally you act as though—what do they say in the cop shows?—anything you say will be used against you. Though,' he added thoughtfully, 'you still get the message across. You have silent disapproval off to a fine art.'

'I have never assumed that anything I have to say would interest you. Now I know we can have nice long cosy chats.'

Her venom made his lips twitch. 'I can hardly wait.'

Alice saw the twitch and her own lips pursed as her eyes continued to linger on his mouth; it was extremely expressive. And sensual, she added, covertly examining the sculpted sexy outline. It was the mouth you expected someone who kissed really well to possess.

Did Luca kiss really well? If practice counted for anything he ought to, she reflected. An indentation appeared to mar the smooth perfection of her broad brow as she considered a small sample of the women he'd practised with. All were stunning, not just good-looking, but the sort of women who turned heads when they walked into a room.

It wasn't until her restless gaze clashed with Luca's that she appreciated how long she'd been sitting there staring at him, thinking about his mouth and kissing! A shamed warmth spread across her skin.

Good God, he's right, I must have had a bit too much to drink! Nothing else could even begin to excuse her behaviour.

She lifted her hand and smiled at the figure who was approaching the table from across the room. 'Here's Seth. Will you *please* try and be nice?' she hissed.

'I'm always nice.'

This was so *not* true that she didn't even bother responding.

CHAPTER THREE

'PROBLEM?' Luca said as the other man approached.

Seth shook his head. "Fraid so. I'm going to have to love you and leave you.'

'Oh, God, no!' Alice flushed deeply when both men turned to look at her. 'That is, we wanted you to stay and eat with us, Seth.' Her glare dared Luca to deny this assertion.

He did.

'We didn't.'

Alice shot Luca a murderous look, and he shrugged, which made her want to shake him. A physical impossibility, of course, considering his size. Not only was Luca tall, but his body had the toned development of an athlete, all lean muscle and whipcord strength.

Her breathing imperceptibly quickened as her eyes slid to his upper body. His jacket was open and she noticed for the first time that there was a slight rent in the expensive fabric through which she could see a section of smooth golden skin.

Normally he was immaculately turned out, not a hair out of place. Was it the minor accident he had lightly touched upon or had some over-zealous lover been a little too eager to remove his clothes?

In her head she saw eager hands ripping at his clothes and her concentration slipped. A secret little shiver of which she was deeply ashamed ran down her spine. Swallowing, she tore her eyes away.

As she turned to the Texan she put a few hundred watts of extra warmth into her smile. '*I'd* love for you to eat with us.'

'And I'd like nothing better,' Seth returned with a rueful sigh.

'Men like a woman to be direct,' her sister, who was happy and married and wanted Alice to be happy again, had explained on her last visit home.

'Direct women scare men off,' her brother, Tom, had corrected.

'Direct women scare *you* off. Men who are not immature and lacking in confidence are not scared by strong women who speak their mind,' her sister replied.

This provocative reply had been the start of a heated discussion. Now seemed as good a time as any to see which of her siblings had been right, despite her not really feeling attracted to Seth.

'Will I see you again?'

Encouraging. Seth looked surprised, but he wasn't running away.

'If you're still here at the end of the week I've got tickets for the opening night of Krebs's exhibition.'

'I'm not totally sure yet how long we'll be in town, but—'

'Roman keeps her pretty busy,' Luca inserted smoothly. His eyes were fixed on the hand laid against the smoother-than-silk contours of Alice's shoulder. As Seth's fingertips brushed casually against the hollow of one collar-bone, which was delicately defined without being unattractively bony, Luca stiffened.

Alice simmered silently. What was it with Luca? Did he begrudge her a social life?

'Ring me.' She softened the abruptness of her demand with a warm smile and added, 'I'd really love to go to the opening although I won't be able to afford to buy anything,' she admitted.

'I'm sure Seth will buy it for you if you look wistful enough,' Luca observed lazily.

Alice's hands clenched into fists under the table.

Luca watched the colour wash over her skin then equally abruptly recede leaving a febrile spot of colour on each smooth cheek. One dark brow lifted.

'Calm down, I was just joking.'

Seth chuckled, apparently having no problem with believing him, but Alice was under no such illusion.

'Of course I'll ring,' Seth promised her. 'You're staying here?'

She nodded, all the while very conscious of heavy-lidded blue eyes watching her.

'Together…?' One brow raised, Seth's speculative look encompassed both Alice and Luca.

It was such an off-the-wall idea that it took several moments for Alice to catch his meaning. When she did her bewildered frown morphed into a look of stark horror. 'Me and…*Luca*?' she squeaked, shaking her head hard in a negative motion to the insulting question.

'You don't fight like friends, more like an old married couple…*or lovers*.'

Alice looked at him as though he were mad. Her own parents rarely raised their voices, let alone fought like cat and dog.

'We don't fight like friends, because we're not.' Trying to tear emotional strips off one another was not to her a sign of a close emotional relationship or for that matter—the thought made her skin heat—a *physical* one!

She turned her head, expecting to find Luca either laughing his socks off at the idea of them being an item or seeing the same revulsion she had experienced reflected on his face.

She found neither.

Luca was still, so still he appeared barely to be breathing. His glossy dark head, which in the candlelight gleamed blue-black, was tilted at an angle so that he appeared to be looking down at her. Through the thick dark mesh of his lashes she could see the gleam of his eyes, but nothing in his facial expression gave a clue as to what he was thinking. A sphinx would have given away more of his feelings than Luca, but the act of looking into those still criminally perfect frozen features set her heart off fibrillating like a wild thing in her chest.

'Sorry, folks, I got the wrong idea.'

Seth's amused apology broke the spell that bound her. 'Yes, you did,' she agreed. Did her smile look as forced as it felt? she wondered. 'Do I look like someone *he* would date?' she demanded in a voice that was the verbal equivalent of a shudder.

Seth appeared to find the question highly amusing. 'I thought maybe Luca here had decided to go for a bit of class for a change.' He slid the younger man a sideways twinkling look of challenge.

'I see you're a believer in miracles,' Alice retorted. 'And a sense of humour, I like that in a man.'

'I'm an easy man to like,' he promised her as he bent forward to kiss her lightly on the cheek. 'I'll be in touch,' he promised. 'Nice to see you again, Luca.'

Watching him go, Alice was suddenly filled with blind panic at the thought of being left alone with Luca, even alone in such a public place!

'I have a sense of humour,' Luca announced from out of the blue.

'No, you have a savage and cutting wit.' As someone who had been on the receiving end often enough, she felt qualified to respond on this score. 'It isn't the same thing,' she promised with feeling.

Luca shrugged but didn't respond to the accusation. 'I thought he'd never go.' He sighed, leaning back in his seat. 'We're ready to order now,' he said to the waiter, who had returned to their table.

'I'm not.' How come when *I* want a waiter there is never one around? 'I'm not hungry.' She was, but she felt like being stubborn.

'Sorry, the lady isn't ready to order…' The waiter nodded and vanished.

'Don't apologise for me,' she retorted spikily. 'You were unconscionably rude to Seth!' she hissed.

'I've had a bad day.'

'My heart bleeds.'

A look of fastidious distaste contorted his aristocratic and fabulously good-looking features. 'And my idea of winding down is *not* watching you and Seth making out,' he revealed.

'We were not making out!' she choked in outrage.

'Talk about all over one another!' he exclaimed in disgust. 'I thought I might have to throw a bucket of water over the pair of you.'

The hand Alice had been threading though her blonde hair fell away as her jaw dropped. It took her several moments to recover the power of speech; when she did her voice shook with anger.

'I won't ask what *your* idea of winding down after a bad day is,' she said with a scornful sniff. Even as she said it her wilful imagination was doing just that. Minus the tie; minus the shirt; minus…! She sucked in her breath and took control before he lost any more garments.

Luca planted his elbows on the table and, with his big body curved towards her, effectively cut out the rest of the room from her view. His breath caused the candles set in the middle of the table to flare and flicker as he planted his chin against the heel of his palm. The action, abrupt but elegantly co-ordinated, made her tummy flip. The feeling was intensified by the illusion they were alone. Luca's every action, even the most mundane, was performed with a fluid, almost animal, grace that was magnetically *male*.

There had been occasions in the past when caught unawares she had seen him walk across a room, knowing even at a distance who it was, and she would watch, helpless not to follow him with her eyes. Those occasions could unsettle her for the rest of day, though generally she succeeded in laughing off her weakness. Right now there was absolutely no question of laughing; he was too close and she was feeling strange.

'Why?' Alice blinked to clear her confused, disorganised

thoughts as eyes deep and drowningly blue locked onto her own. 'Afraid you might discover we both like to wind down the same way?'

His taunt, low-pitched and huskily intimate, sent a shiver rippling through her body. Though she had no control over the heat that spilled out across her pale skin, pride stopped her lowering her eyes in confusion.

'That I seriously doubt.' Her scornful response wasn't quite as scornful as she'd have liked, which had more than a little to do with the images of him *unwinding* her overexcited imagination was predictably supplying.

If he had even the faintest inkling…?

Luca's eyes scoured her faintly flushed face and slowly the corners of his beautiful mouth lifted.

Inkling, girl…? It's written all over your face.

Mortified by her fatal weakness, Alice arranged her features in a careful blank canvas.

With a shrug of his broad shoulders Luca leaned back in his seat. 'What do you think Roman would say if he knew you went around picking up stray men in hotel bars?'

'Roman…?' She imagined that he would say *go for it*. Her boss was always complaining that she had no social life. According to him it made him feel guilty—not guilty enough to cut down on her workload, she had been tempted to retort.

'By the way, nice going with Seth.'

Alice gave a suspicious frown.

'You didn't know Seth's father owned half of Texas and he's an only child?'

It wasn't hard to see where he was going with this one. 'No, I didn't,' she gritted back.

'One of life's lucky chances,' he mused.

'It's true!' Alice hissed in frustration. She was hard pressed to decide which made her most mad: being called promiscuous or a gold-digger? Only *Luca* could manage to do both in the same sentence!

She focused on a point over his shoulder. 'Naturally now I do I will propose at the first opportunity.'

'I'm sure you wouldn't be so obvious.'

'A compliment...*gosh*! Also, this isn't a bar.' The cutting retort would have been more cutting if it hadn't taken her thirty seconds to think of it.

'*Semantics*: the last refuge of the guilty,' Luca suggested gently.

Alice took a deep breath and refused to take the bait. Unless you kept your wits about you when talking to Luca it took him about six seconds to tie a person in knots. 'And I did not pick Seth up.' She was quite pleased with herself for staying firmly focused.

'A moderately clever woman doesn't have to, she makes the poor dope think it was his idea.'

'I'm assuming when you talk about *clever*, you actually mean animal cunning of the variety that men like you assume all women have. You know, I had no idea that you were such a misogynist.' There was a fatal flaw in her coping strategy of focusing on a point over his shoulder—there was only so long she could keep it up!

Her eyes clashed with Luca's and she spoilt her clever rebuttal by adding in a loud, goaded voice, 'Oh, shut up!'

Colouring pinkly, she gave the couple at the next table an apologetic smile before turning her attention back to her persecutor.

'I didn't open my mouth.'

If she'd had the energy the innocence in his protest would have made her smile, but she felt totally drained. Talking to him was exhausting! As she tried to marshal her wits her eyes slid of their own volition to the sculpted outline of the lips he had referred to...

'But you were about to.'

He bowed his dark head in mocking acknowledgement.

'I knew this evening was going to be awful, I just didn't know *how* awful. And for the record if I had picked up Seth it wouldn't have had anything to do with his bank balance.'

'I didn't have you down as a girl with a thing for cowboy boots.'

A hissing sound of annoyance escaped through Alice's clenched teeth.

'It depends who's wearing them,' she rallied.

'Should I take that remark personally?'

'By all means,' she replied with a smile as insincere as his own. 'What's wrong, Luca? Are you feeling bitter and twisted because the girls are interested in your bank balance and not the *real* you? *Poor Luca!*'

Poor Luca gave her a smile that was one hundred per cent cynical charisma. 'You care—I'm touched, I really am.'

'In the head,' she muttered.

His lips twitched. 'Actually,' he explained, 'I tend to find it's my body that interests them most.'

'Just as I thought, you've started believing your own press releases,' she said. 'I'd be surprised if any of the women in that terrible article could spell their own name.'

'*Harsh!* How about sisterly solidarity? After all, you obviously read that *terrible* article too. Which terrible article was it we were talking about? There are so many,' he sighed.

The small gurgling sound of inarticulate disgust that emerged from her throat caused his wolflike grin to widen, revealing a perfect set of whiter-than-white teeth.

'Being a sex object is a burden, but...' another of his inimitable Latin shrugs '...I can live with it.'

Alice didn't respond. It wasn't easy; her facial muscles ached, as did the scream of sheer aggravation locked in her throat. It came so easily to him, she thought with frustration, all the sexual stuff that had every woman within a five-mile radius panting.

But not me!

Desperation and defiance...roughly a sixty-forty split? the ironic voice in her head suggested.

'Your fortitude and sense of duty does you credit, I'm sure.'

Infuriatingly he seemed to find her malice amusing.

'And for the record if I had decided to *pick up* Seth or, for that matter, anyone else,' she continued indignantly, 'I wouldn't care what you or Roman thought, because, strange as it might seem to you, working for an O'Hagan doesn't preclude having a personal life!' She lifted her hand to her mouth to cut off an unexpected yawn.

His all-encompassing gaze scanned her pale features. 'Tired?'

Holding his eyes, she placed the napkin she had been systematically folding and unfolding in her lap on the table. 'Extremely tired of this conversation.'

It wasn't until she actually got to her feet—thank God they didn't fold under her—that she knew what she was doing. She was doing something she ought to have done hours ago… getting the hell out of there! It wasn't in her nature to run from a fight. Her normal response to a difficult situation was to grit her teeth and tough it out, but this was one fight she couldn't win.

Luca's forceful personality she could deal with; it was his raw, rampant sexuality that she couldn't. Trying to maintain a semblance of normality when her imagination was busy spinning erotic fantasies was a humiliating experience. The unpalatable fact was she could fight Luca, but could no longer fight herself and the way he made her feel.

'So if you'll excuse me…' The longer she stayed, the more she would have to regret tomorrow.

His lean face was a study of astonishment as she got to her feet. 'What if I say I won't excuse you?'

'It will make no difference whatever,' she informed him simply before walking away, head held high, back straight. She got as far as the foyer before he caught her up at the same time as the effects of the stress of the evening from hell. She was literally shaking with reaction.

'I assumed I was meant to follow you.'

Alice stopped dead. It had been a terrible evening and this was the final straw. She hadn't retreated to get his attention, just to retain a little sanity. Dear God, Luca had a treble dose of male vanity.

Eyes narrowed, she swung to face the figure at her shoulder. Looking into his face meant she had to tilt her head back a long way. 'No, you're not supposed to follow.'

'Sorry, I'm a bit hazy on the rules governing women storming out.' The muscles along his taut jaw clenched. 'Not many women have stormed out of a restaurant on me…actually, none have.'

So that was his problem—*pride*. His precious ego couldn't take a woman walking out on him. Anger sent a rush of adrenaline through her body.

'Great, my place in history is assured. The woman who walked out on Luca O'Hagan. It doesn't get much better than that—except possibly being remembered as the woman who cured cancer, but still…' She lifted a hand to her aching throat as a shaky little laugh was drawn from it. 'Do you think they'll write a book about me?'

'I think they'll…' He drew in a shuddering breath through flared nostrils and glared down at her, his imperious features clenched into a tight mask of displeasure. 'That smart mouth of yours is going to get you into trouble one of these days,' he predicted grimly.

'Maybe. Then again, maybe it could also get me out of trouble. But then I forget—you prefer brute force, don't you?'

'I have not been fighting.'

'Whatever. I really couldn't care. Before I go to bed I'd like to get a couple of things straight. Three things, actually. Firstly, that wasn't storming, that was a dignified exit.'

'I stand corrected,' he conceded with a stiff bow of his dark head.

'Secondly, they may not have stormed out but—trust me— some must have wanted to, and thirdly…' She stopped. 'Actually there is no thirdly,' she admitted lamely.

She was too startled to resist when Luca suddenly caught her arm and drew her towards him. She opened her mouth to protest when she saw why he'd grabbed her. Though God knew how she hadn't noticed until now the laughing party of hotel guests in celebratory mood heading for the bar—they were making enough noise.

Luca, who muttered something harsh in Italian under his breath, made no attempt to move out of their path as they surged forward, but then she reflected he didn't need to. Luca was not the sort of person that anyone who wasn't insane or stupid jostled. *Or walked away from?* He had looked very angry.

Actually he still did.

As she looked at his fingers curled around her wrist she felt an enervating wave wash over her. The temptation not to fight it but to go with the flow was immense.

'I don't appreciate being…' A small grunt of pain escaped her lips as she received a glancing blow from an elbow in the ribs.

'Are you all right?' She angrily brushed away Luca's hand.

'I'm so sorry, I didn't see you there.' The woman she stepped back into looked concerned.

'I'm fine. It was my fault, I wasn't looking. Don't worry about it.'

'Are you sure?'

'Absolutely.' The fixed smile was still on her lips when the woman moved away.

Luca stood motionless while a shocking realisation swept over him.

He had chased after a woman.

Never in his life had he chased after a woman, but if he had done he didn't think it was too off the wall, too unrealistic to think that she might have been flattered! Any other woman but this one.

Luca waited until the middle-aged woman had moved out of earshot, waited until he could trust himself to speak calmly before he spoke.

'Well, far be it from me to inflict myself on you.' With a curt nod he turned back towards the dining room.

'Luca, I need to get outside—*now*!'

CHAPTER FOUR

IT WAS the hoarse, haunted note in Alice's barely audible voice that made Luca turn back.

'What's wrong? Are you ill?' He watched as she moistened her pallid lips with the tip of her tongue. The cold impatience in his eyes morphed into concern when he realised that every vestige of colour had gone from her face and her skin was covered in a thin film of moisture.

Alice shook her head. It required every ounce of her will-power to make her numb lips work. 'I just need some fresh air…now…*please*…'

She was looking straight at him but there was no recognition in her wide eyes. Just stark, chilling horror.

'Are you hurt? Alice, say something.'

Alice could hear her name and she tried desperately to respond. 'I think I'll just…' She began to lift one foot at a time but they felt as if they were nailed to the ground. Her knees shook with the effort to support her weight.

She could see Luca's lips moving but the words coming from his mouth made no sense. She had no ability to control the relentless kaleidoscope of images that flashed across her vision. Fear was a metallic taste in her mouth. She lifted a hand to her head and felt the clammy wetness of cold sweat.

It was happening again.

The doctor had given *it* a name. He had diagnosed post-traumatic stress disorder.

'But I haven't had a trauma,' she had replied, confident he must have the wrong notes laid out on the desk in front of him. This was the sort of thing that happened when you couldn't get an appointment with your usual doctor.

The doctor had looked quizzically at her over the top of his trendy designer spectacles. 'You were the victim of a knife attack, I understand? And you were also widowed…how long…?'

'My husband died some years ago,' she told him quietly. 'And the attack was a long time ago.' In the time since she had never awoken in the night in a blind panic. She had not suffered any flashbacks. She shook her head. 'Why should this be happening now?'

'Who knows?'

'Well, I rather hoped you would,' she returned drily.

The medic grinned. 'Good to see you've still got a sense of humour,' he commended heartily. 'I'm not an expert, but,' he added, handing her a card, 'I know someone who is. It's not unusual for this to happen some time after the event, years sometimes…a trigger, stress perhaps?'

'I'm not stressed—at least I wasn't until this started happening. I'm not sleeping.' She swallowed; the truth was she was afraid to sleep. 'It has happened twice now when I'm at work. I'm not sure how long I can hide it,' she admitted worriedly.

'And it's necessary for you to hide it? Your employer would not be sympathetic?' he probed.

'I don't want his sympathy…' Or, and which was more to the point, his guilt! It had been bad enough before. The way Roman had gone on after she'd come out of hospital, you'd have thought he had wielded the knife himself.

If her boss, with his overdeveloped sense of responsibility, ever got a sniff of her new problem he'd go off on another mammoth guilt trip and that was something Alice wanted to avoid at all costs. The hair-shirt period, while it lasted, had been pretty wearing, being considerate and reasonable just wasn't in Roman's nature!

'And I really don't want to involve anyone else,' she announced firmly.

'You might have no choice,' the doctor replied bluntly. 'This could get worse before it gets better,' he explained cheerily. He saw her expression. 'Then again…'

'It might not,' she finished heavily.

He shrugged.

'So actually you have no idea.'

The doctor continued to be frustratingly vague. 'It's not an exact science. The human mind is complex.'

'That doesn't help me much.'

'I could arrange that referral for you now if you like?' he suggested.

Alice got to her feet. 'Actually it might be better if I got back to you on that. I'll be out of the country for the next few weeks and—'

'There is no stigma attached to having therapy, Miss Trevelyan.'

Alice smiled. She had seen the address on the card; Harley Street did not come cheap. 'Don't worry, I'll get back to you after I've checked my diary.'

She didn't. Even if she could have afforded it the idea of a stranger poking around in her subconscious did not appeal to Alice. Weren't therapists for people who didn't have friends to talk to?

Alice had friends, but she didn't burden them with her problem; instead she looked up post-traumatic stress on the internet. Armed with as much information as any 'expert', she felt sure she could cope without resorting to therapists.

The turning point had been discovering what the trigger was. Sounds or even smells had been known to trigger attacks, this particular article had explained. In her case it had been an expensive bottle of perfume that she had received for her birthday…the same perfume Roman's stalker had been doused in! The woman whom she had just collided with also wore it.

If she had caught on sooner she could have saved herself weeks of the flashbacks and awful episodes of inescapable blind, brain-numbing panic when her heart pounded as though it would implode and her body was bathed in a cold sweat. But who could know that a bottle of perfume of all things could be the culprit?

'Can you walk?'

She turned her head towards the voice; it came from some distant point above her head. 'Maybe.'

'*Madre di Dio*. I'm getting a doctor.'

'No…don't.' She took a deep breath. 'Sorry. Yes…yes, I can walk. It's passing.'

Luca's dark features clenched as he looked into the stricken, waxily pale face of the woman who stood swaying before him. She looked as though she was going to collapse.

He shook his head. 'I'm getting that doctor.'

'I don't need a doctor.' She gripped his arm tightly as the room tilted. 'Please, Luca,' she pleaded. 'I just need some fresh air and I'll be fine.'

Her relief when he slipped an arm around her waist was profound. With a sigh she sagged against him. 'Thank you. I'm very sorry to be a bother,' she murmured, tucking her head against his shoulder.

At the top of the sweep of elegant steps that led up to the entrance Luca gave up on the pretence he *wasn't* actually carrying her and scooped her up into his arms.

'You're shaking like a leaf,' he discovered as her soft curves melded into his hard angles. 'I knew I should have called that doctor.' His eyes darkened with self-recrimination; he had allowed her irrational pleas to influence his better judgement.

'Please don't do that, Luca.' Luca looked from the wide blue eyes to the small hand that tightened on his sleeve and back again. Somewhere from the muddled mess of her thoughts a realisation that she was being carried for the second time in her life by Luca O'Hagan emerged.

'You're always around when I need carrying. Only twice in my life…obviously I'm not counting when I was a baby…' She just managed to bite off the flow of confidences before she revealed that he smelt extremely good.

'You're not a baby now.' The creature in his arms was all woman.

'Am I talking rubbish?'

'No more than usual.'

'Good.'

'I'm too heavy.'

'For what?' Under normal circumstances Alice might have taken note and wondered at his oddly thickened tone.

'For you.' Arms like steel bands effortlessly stilled her uncoordinated feeble struggles. 'I can walk.' It didn't necessarily mean she wanted to.

The lean brown fingers that framed her jaw left her no choice but to look up into the face of the man who held her.

'And even if you couldn't you'd prefer to fall flat on your face than let me carry you.' Eyes as keen as a laser and equally objective scanned her face. Whatever he saw must have satisfied him because he gave a grudging grunt and then set her down on the pavement.

Alice stood there taking big greedy gulps of fresh air while he arranged his jacket around her smooth bare shoulders. She was outside in the street and had only the vaguest memory of the events that had got her there.

'Right, you're not going to faint on me, are you?' he asked suspiciously.

'No, of course not.'

'There's no of course about it.'

Her glance dropped evasively from his searching scrutiny. 'I felt a little light-headed. I'm fine now,' she said, injecting a strained note of false cheer into her voice. 'You go back and have your dinner,' she suggested. 'I'll take a little stroll.' She had barely begun to shrug off his jacket when two heavy hands landed on her shoulders, effectively anchoring it there.

'You have taken *stupid* to an entirely new level.' Luca, being Luca, didn't see the need to lower his voice and several people looked at them; a few stopped and stared.

'Please,' Alice hissed with an agonised look over her shoulder. 'People are looking at us. Let's walk.' Walking at least they might blend in a little. When he didn't respond she caught hold of his hand. 'Come on,' she urged.

For a moment she thought he wasn't going to co-operate, then suddenly his fingers closed around hers. Her eyes widening as a tingling sexual shock sizzled through her body, she almost missed a step, but somehow carried on walking as though nothing had happened.

There was something quite surreal about it; she was walking hand in hand down the street with Luca O'Hagan. They were still hand in hand when the flashes started popping. Without thinking, Alice turned her head into Luca's chest. He held her there until he said, in what seemed to her an amazingly disinterested fashion, 'He's gone.' Her face was framed between big hands. 'You all right? You've got a bit more colour in your face.'

'I'm fine. What was that?'

'A photographer.'

'Why was he taking our photo?'

'I would imagine that it was to go with the one of me carrying you out of the hotel he took.'

'Oh, my God!' She angled a worried look at his profile. 'Will it be in a newspaper?' She hated the idea, but took comfort from the fact that at least there was very little chance of anyone she knew seeing it.

'Almost certainly.'

'I suppose you could explain to them that I was ill?'

Luca slid her an incredulous look. 'They'll assume you were drunk.'

On this occasion she couldn't work up enough indignation to complain that he was talking to her as if she were a child.

'That's the worst-case scenario…right?'

'No, them suggesting you were under the influence of illegal substances is the worst-case scenario.'

Alice would have fallen had his arm not shot out to steady her. 'But I wasn't. I'd had just a few drinks…and I've never…I don't do stuff like that.'

'You think the fact that it's not true will stop them printing it? *Dio mio*, what planet have you been living on, *cara*?'

'This is terrible. I'm so…so sorry. This is all my fault,' she said, chewing fretfully on her lower lip.

'Don't be stupid, it's nobody's fault. Unless you tipped him off that I'd be carrying a woman out of that particular hotel this evening?'

'Why would I do that?'

His sensual mouth twisted as he recognised the genuine bewilderment in her wide blue eyes. 'You'd be surprised,' he returned cryptically. 'It was just a lucky break for him. Don't stress.'

Easy for him to say, she thought. He was used to seeing his face plastered across newspapers.

He led her across the street. 'In case you were wondering, that was me being sympathetic and soothing.' He smiled into her startled eyes and urged her forward. 'Come on, it's at the next intersection.'

'What is?'

'Where we're heading.'

'Are we heading somewhere?' Silly question. Luca didn't aimlessly wander, he always had an aim and objective. And with his single-minded focus and determination he inevitably achieved it, she reflected.

'I didn't get my dinner and you haven't eaten for three weeks,' he reminded her wryly. 'I know this great little Italian.'

'I can't let you buy me dinner,' she protested immediately.

'Saying no to anything I suggest is like a reflex with you, isn't it?' The corners of Luca's wide, mobile mouth lifted as he watched her open her mouth and close it again with a grimace. 'And anyway,' he added, 'who says I'm buying?'

Her lashes came down in a screen. 'But that's not what I meant…'

'I know,' he cut back impatiently.

A frown puckered her brow as she fretted. 'If Roman finds out you've bought me dinner somewhere he's going to think it's really odd.' He wouldn't be the only one.

'And do you normally ask my brother's permission before you go out on a date with someone?'

'Of course I don't,' she denied. Her frown deepened—surely he could see what she meant? 'It's just that it's—*you*.' She stopped abruptly, the colour rushing attractively to her cheeks. 'Obviously I know this isn't a date!' she added, anxious to let him know that she wasn't making any daft assumptions.

'*Obviously*,' he echoed as dry as dust.

She glanced up to see his expression was…well, actually he didn't have an expression. Despite this absence of anything she couldn't shake the feeling she had said something to make him mad.

'So now that we're in agreement on something,' he continued in the same tight, controlled voice, 'why don't you do us both a favour and just do as you're told? Just this once.'

'What happened to sympathetic and soothing?'

There was a perceptible thawing in his manner as his eyes brushed her indignant face. 'I'm cranky when I'm not fed,' he confessed.

'You're cranky full stop,' she retorted, happy if not relieved to accept this explanation for his intense mood.

'And when I've fed you,' he continued in a conversational tone, 'you can tell me what happened back there.'

Alice, caught off guard, stiffened. 'What happened back there?' she echoed, feigning ignorance.

Bad enough, she thought, inwardly cringing at the memory of him carrying her out of the hotel, to have made such an exhibition of herself in front of him, without going into the details. She couldn't imagine for a second that anyone as strong and seemingly invulnerable as Luca would not despise weakness in others.

'I can see how looking as though you'd just seen your worst nightmare and then almost losing consciousness might slip your mind, especially when it happened—what…?' He consulted his wrist-watch. 'Almost ten minutes ago,' he drawled.

'There is no need to be sarcastic.'

'Wrong, there is every need to be sarcastic…being sarcastic is the only thing stopping me from ki…strangling you.'

For a split second Alice had thought he was going to say kissing…*now how delusional was that*?

'Maybe I had too much to drink, but as you can see I'm fine now.' She gave a brilliant smile just to illustrate how fine she was.

Luca inhaled and closed his eyes. 'Clearly it was all a figment of my imagination.'

His scorching sarcasm made her wince. 'I've already explained.'

Expressive hands spread out before him in a dismissive gesture, Luca nodded, his face taut with annoyance. 'Let's just leave it, shall we?'

Alice, who was more than ready to leave it, gave a nod of sheer relief. She supposed that he did have some justification for being annoyed. She had gone out of her way to be unpleasant to him—something she might have to think about at a later date…*much* later—made him miss dinner, and he couldn't be too happy about the prospect of explaining away tomorrow's newspapers to the sublime Ingrid. Thoughts of the sublime Ingrid sent her fragile spirits plummeting.

The entrance to the tiny Italian restaurant was down a side street. 'Careful of the stairs—they're steep,' Luca warned as he preceded her down the steep flight. Presumably if she slipped he was going to cushion her fall.

Some people might think it worth a few bruises to land on top of Luca O'Hagan.

She took great care with the steps.

The interior of the unprepossessing building proved to be totally charming. The cosy room, decorated in a delightfully rustic style, was filled with warmth and laughter…and *people*! Lots of people! The place was literally heaving and the diners, like the mismatched and eccentric crockery, were a pretty assorted bunch, some dressed down in casual jeans, others dressed up to the nines.

There was absolutely no way they were going to get a table this side of midnight.

'It looks full,' she said as Luca slid the jacket off her shoulders.

'I'm sure they'll squeeze us in somewhere,' Luca responded with what seemed to Alice like wildly misplaced optimism.

'You're too big to squeeze in,' she retorted, her critical gaze lighting on his broad shoulders. Her stomach took an unscheduled dive. 'We might as well leave,' she added hurriedly.

'We've only just arrived.'

'You obviously have to book.' She sighed wistfully as a plate of something that looked and smelt delicious was placed in front of some lucky diners. Alice realised just how hungry she was. 'This is too cruel,' she complained.

Two minutes later they were sitting at a table for two in a concealed alcove. They couldn't have treated Luca with more warmth had he been the proverbial returning black sheep or visiting royalty. The owner, Paolo, who had kissed her soundly on both cheeks when Luca had introduced her, had taken their orders himself.

Not that she had had the opportunity to place her order; Luca had taken the unseen menu from her hand and handed it back to Paolo.

'We'll leave it up to you. That's all right with you, is it, Alice?'

Alice hadn't been left with much option but to nod.

As they were so busy Alice was resigned to a long wait, but

about two seconds later a pretty girl who looked like a female version of one of the waiters appeared. 'Sorry to keep you waiting.'

'Do I detect a family resemblance?' Alice asked after she had deposited their meals in front of them.

'This is very much a family business; Gina is Paolo's granddaughter.'

'How do you know them so well?' Or was it just the pretty Gina he knew well? 'They don't seem like your…' She stopped and shook her head. 'They seem really nice and this,' she added brightly, 'looks delicious.'

Unfortunately Luca wasn't going to let her off the hook.

'They don't look like my what, Alice? My sort of people?' he suggested.

She coloured but didn't respond to his angry undertone. 'What *are* my sort of people? You think I'm some sort of élitist snob, don't you?'

She lifted her eyes from her plate. The conflict that she felt was tearing her apart was reflected in her troubled eyes. 'To be honest I don't know what you are,' she admitted with a spurt of candour. 'You're confusing.' Or should that be I'm confused?

For a long moment he looked into her face. Then with one of the startling changes of mood he was capable of he grinned. A wide, incredibly charismatic grin that split his face. 'The first time I came in here I ended up washing the dishes.'

Alice's eyes were round with astonishment. '*You!*'

'I'd had my wallet lifted and I didn't discover it until I came to pay,' he explained. 'Paolo gave me a choice: the cops or the washing-up,' he recalled.

'You chose the washing-up?'

He nodded, looking amused by her open-mouthed astonishment.

Alice, her food forgotten, put down her fork. 'But the police would have been able to confirm that you weren't a con man,' she protested.

'I know.'

'Then why?'

'I hadn't been in the city for long and I didn't know many people. Actually…' his eyes held a gleam of self-mockery as they lifted from the prolonged contemplation of the ruby-red liquid in his glass '—I think it's possible I was lonely.'

Alice shook her head. 'You're teasing!' she accused. The idea of Luca O'Hagan washing up was hard enough to get her head around, but him being lonely! 'You expect me to believe you were reduced to sitting in your hotel room watching repeats on the television?'

Luca, who didn't immediately respond, leaned back in his chair and watched the play of expression across her flushed face. 'Haven't you ever felt lonely in the middle of a room of people, Alice?'

'Yes, I have,' she admitted, too startled by the soft question to prevaricate. 'But you're not—' She broke off, flushing in face of his sardonic smile.

'Capable of experiencing the same feelings you do, Alice?'

Alice, who felt there had been far too much discussion of feelings tonight, changed the subject. 'I don't expect your date was too pleased when you decided to wash up.'

'I didn't have a date that night.'

She picked up her fork. 'That was lucky.'

'Actually you're the first woman I've ever brought here,' he revealed, before turning his attention to the neglected food before them. 'Right,' he urged. 'Eat up. Paolo makes the best *fritto misto di pesce* in town and he'll be offended if you don't clear your plate.'

As Alice began to fork the fried fish, which was every bit as delicious as Luca had contended, into her mouth her thoughts were otherwise engaged. *No other woman*…that was what he had said. Of course she'd be daft to read anything into that…all the same…

CHAPTER FIVE

'I'M BEGINNING to feel a good deal of empathy for the animals in the zoo...'

Luca, his expression perplexed, shook his head.

'At feeding time,' Alice elucidated and he grinned.

That grin totally transformed the classically severe cast of lean features, banishing the stony reticence she was used to, and lending it an attractive warmth.

It was the most relaxed she had ever seen him, Alice realised. Her eyes flickered briefly to the discarded tie casually flung over the back of his chair and his elbows planted on the table. The steel had gone from his spine and the scorn from his expression as he slouched elegantly in his chair.

This was Luca with the charm and vigour but minus the snootiness and sneers—in short a pretty irresistible proposition.

'I like watching you eat; most women pick at their food.'

'Whereas I fall on it and devour it like a ravening beast?' she suggested, pushing aside the last portion on her plate with a regretful sigh. 'I feel so special...or should that be freaky?'

'Settle for different,' he suggested.

Her shoulders lifted. 'I can live with that,' she agreed amicably.

'What about that last bit?' he asked, pointing at the amount she had left on her plate.

'I'm not being polite. If I eat any more I'll burst. *Messy*,' she said with a grimace.

His mobile mouth quivered. 'Paolo will be hurt,' he contended.

'Fine, you eat it, then,' she suggested with a laugh as she speared a piece of squid onto her fork and held it out to him.

The smile died from his incongruously azure eyes as they collided with her own. In the space of a heartbeat the temperature soared by several degrees. She instantly responded to his abrupt change of mood and would have dropped the fork had his hand not come up to cover her own. Inside his fingers her hand was shaking as, without breaking contact with her wide eyes, he brought the fork up to his mouth.

A tidal wave of blind, uncontrolled lust swallowed her up like some heavy downy duvet. She didn't even try to fight it. Every cell in her body was tuned to him: his voice, his touch…the faint male scent that rose from his warm skin. He leaned across the table and she felt her skin prickle damply with heat.

'Delicious.' His voice was as velvety smooth as the sauce that had covered their food and infinitely more wicked.

Alice was mortified to recognise the low moan issued from her own throat. Luca heard and his eyes darkened dramatically; she felt his fingers spasm around her own.

'Alice.' He swallowed, the muscles in his brown throat visibly spasming. 'I think we both—'

'You enjoyed.' Paolo, oblivious to the atmosphere, beamed at them both. 'Now,' he announced grandly, 'you shall try my *pesche ripiene al forno.*'

Luca's hand withdrew. 'Baked stuffed peaches,' he explained for Alice's benefit.

'Oh, I couldn't. But they sound delicious,' she added quickly when Paolo looked crestfallen. If Paolo wasn't such an attentive host…another couple of minutes and they might have been in another place. Maybe it was just as well that he had interrupted. It was all very well to say she was a free agent, but this didn't alter the fact she still *felt* married. Look how guilty she felt simply acknowledging how attracted she was to Luca!

I'm not ready, she thought.

When their voluble host had gone Luca showed no inclination to take up where he'd left off; his manner was distant and he seemed to have something on his mind. Whereas earlier they had been talking non-stop, now there were inhibiting silences. Several times as she drank her coffee she caught Luca looking at her.

'I think I'd like to go now,' she said finally.

'Alice…'

She tensed expectantly as he dragged a hand through the thick glossy hair he wore longer than was fashionable.

'You were…' He stopped and inhaled deeply. 'Are you planning on seeing Seth again?'

'Seth?' She shook her head, then shrugged. 'I suppose so.'

'Then it doesn't bother you that he's married…or maybe you didn't know?'

Alice's eyes widened, her expression growing defensive as Luca surveyed her sternly from under the sweep of those preposterously sexy eyelashes of his with a look that said she was either a callous home-breaker or a total dope who believed any tale spun by a half-plausible stranger.

Not a person given to physical violence, she suddenly wanted to throw something at him.

'I think he did mention it…' She made a show of frowning as though she was trying to recall something and then smiled. 'Yes…Susan.' She directed a frowning look of enquiry at his taut face. 'Isn't that his wife's name?'

His expression remained veiled, but despite this he managed to project a silent but strong aura of disapproval. 'Yes, it is.'

'You've met her, then?' He acknowledged this with a curt nod. 'Is she very pretty?'

'Very,' he told her shortly.

Alice, who had been counting down from ten, reached four before he exploded.

'The fact he is married makes no difference to you?'

She affected surprise; she must have done it well because she heard the sound of his teeth grinding.

'Should it? It makes no difference to Seth,' she pointed out reasonably.

While Seth had discussed his marriage breakup she had wondered what it was about her that made men feel they could confide their emotional problems. Natural empathy, or did they think of her as a universal agony aunt? She supposed she should find the fact that Luca automatically assumed she was a tart with ulterior motives refreshing.

Presumably Luca didn't like the idea of his friend getting involved with a mere secretary. Ironically he needn't have bothered; Seth was nice, really nice, but she'd known within two minutes of being in his company that there was no spark between them. It wasn't that she was expecting a thunderclap when she saw *the one*, but it stood to reason in her mind that there had to be some chemistry from the first moment for love to stand a chance of developing.

'Have you no concept of self-respect?'

Alice could no longer disguise her feelings under a calm exterior. Her eyes flashed wrathful fire as she pinned him with a contemptuous glare.

'This amount of sanctimonious claptrap coming from a man who sees nothing wrong in seducing his own brother's girl-friend is rich…really rich.'

'Ingrid?' He threw back his head and laughed.

For a moment Alice was distracted from her objective by this inappropriate display of mirth. 'You think it was funny?' she condemned coldly.

'I think it was bloody hilarious,' he told her with eyes as cold as blue steel. 'But we're not talking about me or Ingrid,' he reminded her grimly.

'No, we wouldn't be, because, although you feel totally free to criticise me you'd be gobsmacked if I passed judgement on the way you live your life. No, we're talking about my total lack of moral fibre and principles, aren't we? A theme I sense is close to your heart!' she finished breathlessly. 'Tell me, Luca, how long is it since you touched base with Seth?'

'How should I know?' He looked impatient.

'How long?' she persisted.

'Six…ten months, maybe?'

What Luca needed was a major dose of humility and Alice decided that she was going to provide it.

'It's probably a little bit more than that because otherwise you would have known that Seth and his *pretty* wife are divorced. She ran off with a French count.'

'*French count!* My God, couldn't Seth do better than that? Mind you, I suppose he didn't need to. Did you always walk around with gullible idiot in neon across your forehead?' The angry finger he viciously dragged across his own forehead left a faint raised weal on his olive skin. 'Or is that a recent development?'

Alice found she couldn't take her eyes off the minor blemish. In truth she couldn't take her eyes off him. Every little detail, every tiny nuance afforded her endless fascination.

'I'm not about to apologise because I don't automatically assume someone's lying to me…unless of course they happen to be called Luca O'Hagan. Your problem is you believe everyone is as deceitful as you are,' she contended scornfully. 'The day I'm as cynical and twisted as you I hope someone's around to tell me to get over myself.'

White around the lips, Luca drew in a deep breath through his clenched teeth. 'Is that a fact?'

'Yes, it is. Besides, it's not the sort of thing Seth would make up, is it? I didn't even know there were any real counts in France,' she admitted. 'But apparently this one is the genuine article and poor Seth feels particularly gutted because she met him at a health-spa break that he arranged as a birthday treat.'

There was a degree of satisfaction in seeing Luca, for once

in his life, look taken aback. But not as much satisfaction as she had expected.

'Are you actually serious?'

'Apparently the divorce was finalised last week.'

'So Seth is on the rebound. Congratulations. I suppose it was inevitable. I mean, if Seth thought that marriage would last for ever he was the only one.'

'I can see exactly why he didn't confide in you,' she snapped in disgust. 'The supportive friend you are not.'

'I can see exactly why he confided in you,' Luca returned. 'A born bleeding heart. A suggestion of a tear in those spaniel eyes and you'd be gagging to comfort him.'

She closed her eyes, almost weeping with anger. 'You are disgusting, crude, vile and if you were sobbing your heart out I wouldn't lift a little finger to comfort you.'

'I'd prefer to be crude than an idiot,' Luca retorted. 'I wouldn't have trusted her as far as I could throw her.'

Alice's outraged glare focused on his lean face. How could anyone be that unfeeling to a friend's tragedy?

'Kick a man when he's down, why don't you? That's just typical of you,' she accused. 'You have all the empathy of a Great White…' And, she decided furiously, he was just as ruthless and single-minded. Actually, now that she thought of it the analogy with the cold-blooded predator was extremely apt. Luca was top of the food chain and he had no natural enemies unless it was his own ego.

'I find it hard to empathise with a man who marries a woman just because she's the woman that every other man wants. She was the original trophy wife. But then Seth likes to own beautiful things, as I'm sure you'll discover.'

'And you'd know this after meeting her, how many times?'

'Just the once.'

'Once! Oh, well, you could write the definitive character analysis, then.'

'She came on to me,' he recalled in a matter-of-fact manner.

Alice blinked. *'She what?'*

'Do you want me to spell it out? She came on to me... made a pass.'

'Surely not!' she exclaimed, shaking her head.

'It has been known to happen,' he inserted drily.

Alice felt nauseous as she imagined the occasions he referred to. 'I meant she was married to your friend.'

He slanted an incredulous look at her face. 'I'm beginning to think you live in some little world all of your own where wives never cheat and everyone lives happily ever after.'

'Are you sure you're not the fantasist here?' she countered angrily. 'The poor woman obviously smiled at you and you assumed that she was offering herself. Why is it,' she asked, rolling her eyes, 'men think that every woman in the world fancies the pants off them?'

'Imagination, Alice, doesn't shove its tongue down your throat and its hand down your trousers.'

'She did?' The cynical sneer on his face deepened as she went bright pink. 'Did you...did you...?'

'Did I take her up on the offer? Actually, no, I don't like aggressive women. And even a total sleaze like me draws the line at sleeping with the wife of a friend. Also I'm allergic to silicone,' he admitted with a faint shudder.

Alice closed her mouth over the impulse to declare her cleavage unenhanced and sighed. 'Poor Seth... Fate is really cruel sometimes.'

'Fate?' Luca echoed. 'The same fate that makes two people's eyes meet across a crowded room?' His contemptuous sneer made Alice wince.

'I suppose you believe that people make their own fate?'

Luca looked at her with unconcealed irritation. 'I don't give a damn what *people* do.'

Alice smiled complacently into his dark, displeased face. 'I'm not wrong, though, am I?' she speculated.

'I can't deny it...Alice, you know me so well.' On any other occasion Alice would have responded to the danger in his silky response, but the extraordinary events of this night had imbued her with a strange recklessness.

She shrugged. 'You can be sarcastic, and I'm sure you *love* the idea of being enigmatic, but, let's face it, you're not exactly the most complicated of men ever to look in the mirror and like what he saw.' She saw the shock register in his electric-blue eyes and added innocently, 'No offence intended.'

The silence that followed his soft, *'Dio mio,'* lasted long enough for some doubts to creep in. He was everything she despised in a man, but was it such a good idea to tell him? Satisfying in the short term as it was, it was probably dangerous in the long term. Luca was not a man who let someone else have the last word!

He didn't.

'It's curious but I've noticed people who are eager to point out the faults of others are less eager to hear about their own. Of course, this doesn't apply in Alice's case because *she's* perfect.' He raised his glass in a mocking salute. 'Let's drink to perfect Alice.'

Alice was too angry to think straight. She was as close to *really* losing her temper as she had been in years.

'I'm well aware I'm not perfect,' she grated with a toss of her head.

'Such modesty.'

Her soft lips tightened at his mocking admiration. 'If we're talking compared with you, the answer is yes.'

Luca gave a very Latin shrug. 'So willing to flaunt it and almost perfect. Well, almost perfect is still much more than most of us can aspire to.'

Alice didn't know how she managed to smile through his satiric drawl when all she wanted to do was slap the smirk off his condescending face. 'It's certainly more than you can aspire to,' she agreed with a sweet smile.

Against his will an appreciative growl of laughter was

wrenched from Luca's throat. 'I don't aspire to perfection; I always find paragons incredibly boring.'

She adopted an air of studied disinterest. 'How lucky that you don't drop off in my company.'

'There's always the possibility Roman was wrong about you. He's hardly what you'd call an objective observer, is he?'

'Well, he knows me a damn sight better than you do,' she retorted angrily.

'Granted. Or at least he *thinks* he does. Roman sees you as his indispensable PA and secretary.'

The dismissive note really got under her skin. In all modesty she was pretty indispensable. She hadn't appreciated until now that, despite all his egalitarian talk and washing dishes, Luca was actually a snob.

'I'm more than that.'

Though his tone was totally devoid of expression, there was unmistakable contempt etched in his dark lean face as he responded. 'I'm quite sure you're much, *much* more. Though maybe not quite as much as you'd like to be?'

The sly insinuation made her cheeks burn; anyone listening in would have automatically assumed that she was out to get her boss. Presumably that was the idea? Angrily she lifted her chin.

'Short of having the man's child,' she said with a soft, provocative laugh, 'I don't see how we could be any closer.'

Alice's provocative little smile faded, to be replaced by an expression of dawning horror. I as good as said I'm sleeping with my boss, and I said it to his brother...*oh, God*...!

She blinked as her eyes locked with Luca's. He really does have the bluest eyes I've ever seen. Blue and angry, *very* angry.

She gave her head a tiny shake; obviously she was not right in the head. It passed the bounds of ridiculous, considering the fact he was going out of his way to be even more insulting than usual, that she was wasting her time admiring the sheer unbelievable blueness of the man's eyes!

'That is, I mean—'

'I really don't need you to draw a diagram.'

Under his tan she saw that Luca had gone pale, and she realised that in her desire to score points she had gone too far. If she didn't want to have the unenviable task of explaining to her boss why she'd basically told his brother they were sleeping together, she had better set the record straight…and fast!

'Look, I don't know why I said that,' she admitted, trying for frank and open and achieving panicky and defensive. 'Any more than I know why you think I've got some sort of crush on your brother. But I'm not sleeping with him.'

To her dismay her earnest words appeared to make no impact on Luca. Her shoulders slumped as the nostrils of his narrow-bridged, masterful nose flared. He continued to act like a man who was having a tough time controlling his feelings.

'Working for Roman is always interesting and stimulating,' she added in a voice tinged with desperation. 'We have a very good working relationship…*professional*,' she emphasised. 'I like and respect your brother.' She swallowed as her voice thickened emotionally. 'But seducing him has never even crossed my mind.'

'You can bet it has crossed his. But you're wasting your time. You know Roman isn't in love with you.'

Alice's jaw dropped; mouth unattractively ajar, she stared back at him with stunned incredulity. The man was quite obviously out of his mind.

'Why do you imagine I'd *want* Roman to be in love with me?' she demanded. The idea was so ridiculous that she began to grin. 'So what am I—some love-struck schoolgirl?'

There was obviously absolutely no point being sincere. He had made up his mind and nothing she said or did was going to change it. 'But you know, now that you've put it in my head I've got to thinking it might be interesting…mmm…' She pressed one finger to the slight cleft in her softly rounded chin and pursed her lips thoughtfully.

'It might be fun. After all, how many secretaries marry their boss? It's an acknowledged career path,' she reminded him. 'I think,' she mused, 'I'll go for something large and flash, ring-wise, that is. I mean, if you've got it, flaunt it, that's what I always say.'

'I'd noticed.' With an insolent half-smile on his mobile lips he perused the voluptuous curves of her upper body. 'So, I expect, has every other man in the place.'

Alice felt her nipples harden into burning life. She had no idea from where she found the strength to remain outwardly oblivious to his stare. Even the creamy contours of the cleavage he was crudely ogling flushed.

Alice's eyes narrowed angrily. 'Are there any family heir-looms locked in a vault somewhere? I've always seen myself in rubies.'

He looked at her for a long simmering moment. 'You're not, are you?'

Alice's eyes lifted from her bare left hand and swallowed. She and Mark had decided that a deposit on a house was more important than an engagement ring. But the night they had become officially engaged Mark had slid a plastic ring from a Christmas cracker on her finger.

'Not...?' she echoed blankly.

'You're not sleeping with Roman.'

She rubbed her bare left hand against her cheek. 'Of course I'm not,' she said, suddenly too weary to argue.

'I always thought...'

'You always thought what?'

He shrugged. 'Forget it,' he advised, gazing abstractly into the distance. He had spent so long wondering if his brother was bedding the most desirable woman he'd ever seen and all he'd had to do was ask.

'You realise that you're no longer off limits.'

Alice, who had been looking around to locate the ladies' room where she intended to lock herself in a cubicle and cry, focused on his face. 'Off limits to what?'

His nostrils quivered and his jaw clenched, drawing evenly toned skin that had a delicious golden sheen tight and revealing achingly perfect bone structure. 'Off limits to me,' he elucidated throatily.

Alice blinked. A flash-flood of heat passed through her body. 'This conversation is getting surreal.'

'You're not sleeping with my brother. Sleep with me.'

'Naturally such an offer is incredibly tempting,' she croaked hoarsely. She watched, her temper simmering gently as he ran a hand over his jaw where a dark fuzz of stubble cast a shadow.

'I assumed it would be.'

'I had no idea that it was an either-or option. If you're not sleeping with one brother you have to sleep with the other.' She pressed her face into her palms and shook her head. 'You really are unbelievable,' she breathed.

He inclined his dark head and smiled. 'Thank you.'

'It wasn't a compliment,' she said, pressing her palms tight together. 'What have I ever done to make you think for one second that I'd want to sleep with you?' she demanded scornfully. His mouth opened and suddenly she knew she didn't want to hear the answer to that question. 'And what,' she added hastily, 'did I ever do to make you think that I'm in love with Roman?'

'You took a knife meant for him. You don't risk your life for someone unless they're something special to you.'

CHAPTER SIX

THE knife had been in her hand when Luca had walked into the room. A knife, a beautiful blonde, and his injured—for all he knew at the time *fatally* injured—brother!

His mind had made the obvious connection.

'Luca, you're late,' Roman hailed him before closing his eyes. He was a deeply alarming shade of grey, but breathing, because Luca could see the rise and fall of his chest.

'Too late for the fun, it would seem,' Luca replied, approaching the beautiful blonde with caution, with several theories, most involving a lover's tiff that had gone *seriously* wrong, running through his mind.

After the initial shock when it didn't function at all, your mind, he discovered, worked very fast. A useful piece of information for anyone who walked into their brother's office looking to take him to the pub for a promised pint and finding a blood bath instead!

Before he could wrestle the nasty-looking weapon from her hand the blonde put it down on the desk with a small grimace. Scarcely acknowledging him, she moved towards Roman, who was standing with his shoulders braced against the wall. He had one gory hand pressed to his face, while blood was seeping through his fingers and dripping down onto his pale shirt.

Luca could see his brother's face remained scarily pale and

his attitude dazed, but the fact his brother was standing was something that he took comfort from.

Luca faced a dilemma: take the knife or protect his brother from a possible second attack. His brother, dazed or not, was a good muscular twelve inches taller than the blonde so he went for the knife. Before he touched it the blonde gave an urgent cry of warning.

'Don't touch—the police will want it for forensics!'

His fingers poised above the blood-stained blade, Luca stopped. *'What?'*

'The police…I've phoned, they're on their way.' She began to fold the cardigan she had removed into a tight wad. Underneath she wore a snug-fitting sleeveless top. It passed through his mind that to notice a woman's body at a moment like this could indicate he was seriously disturbed.

The woman with the incredible figure scanned his face suspiciously. 'Look, if you've got a thing about blood maybe you should wait outside,' she suggested kindly.

'Wait outside?' he echoed.

'The last thing we need is you fainting.'

Luca, who had never been treated as though he was not just incompetent and irrelevant, but actually a bit of a nuisance too, was at a loss to know how to respond to this brutally frank observation.

'I won't faint.'

She looked mollified but not convinced. 'I'm glad to hear it.'

'Look, just who the hell…what the hell?' So she might not have attacked his brother, but someone had and he wanted to know who and why!

Her head turned, causing her silvery blonde curls to bounce attractively around her slender shoulders. There was a definite edge of irritation in her voice as she replied.

'Not *now*. And it's probably not a good idea for us to touch anything at all if we can help it.'

From this comment he deduced that she had decided that he looked stupid enough to go around contaminating the crime scene. Before he had thought of a response her attention had moved on. To his injured brother.

'Roman, let me look at it. Sitting down is good,' she added as he slid gracefully down the wall. She knelt beside him. 'That's it, great,' she approved encouragingly as his hand lifted.

'Bad?' Roman asked.

At that moment Luca saw for the first time where most of the blood was coming from.

'*Dio*…your face, Roman!' he exclaimed, shocked by the sight of the deep cut that stretched from just below his brother's eye and extended halfway along his cheekbone.

'It's not nearly as bad as it looks.' The blonde had tilted her head to look at the gaping wound from several angles and said with an approving nod, 'No, not too bad at all.'

'*Not too bad!*' His brother was going to be scarred for life.

A look from those clear blue eyes silenced him. 'It's a good clean cut, which shouldn't leave much of a scar once it heals,' she announced in a tone that didn't invite debate.

At the time Luca hadn't believed her though for Roman's sake he hadn't said so, but in fact time had proved her prediction correct. His brother had been left with an interesting though not disfiguring scar, which the ladies found attractive.

'I'm going to press this against it, Roman, to stop the blood. I'm sorry if it hurts.'

'Go ahead, *cara*.' Roman smiled weakly. 'You all right?'

'I think so.' Her face creased in concentration as she applied the makeshift dressing to his cheek. 'It's not sterile but it is clean.' From her tone and attitude you'd have been forgiven for assuming she was engaged in selling jam at a village fête, not knee-deep in blood and knives!

'Luca, did you see her?'

Luca tore his gaze from the spookily composed blonde. 'See who, her?' he asked ungrammatically.

'My stalker.'

'You have a stalker?'

'Doesn't everyone? You could say she cut and ran. Ouch!' he protested as the blonde applied some extra pressure to his bleeding wound.

'You shouldn't talk so much,' she reproached, huskily stern.

The huskiness and tiny catch were the only indications Luca had picked up so far that suggested maybe she wasn't as cool, calm and collected as she appeared.

'Luca, this is Alice, my assistant. Alice, this is my brother, Luca. You've not met, have you?'

'No.'

'Yes.'

They both spoke in unison.

'That is no,' Luca corrected himself.

What else could he say? You couldn't expect to be taken seriously if you said that you had recognised a person from a lavishly illustrated book your mother had read bedtime stories to you from when you were a child.

But he had.

The blonde curls, the heart-shaped face, the big blue eyes and rosebud lips…she *was* the princess in the tower, only in the flesh she didn't look as if she would hang around waiting for a passing prince to rescue her.

It had been his favourite story.

Luca had recognised straight off that this princess was a different proposition entirely. He was looking at a princess who would not only organise her own escape plan, but put together the most competitively priced package and bring in the project on time!

'What shall I do?' It went against the grain not to take charge, but when all was said and done Roman's bolshy princess secretary seemed to have things in hand.

Actually he didn't get to do anything because just then the police, closely followed by a team of paramedics, arrived. They were quick and efficient.

They looked disappointed when he admitted he'd not witnessed anything, but perked up considerably when Roman's princess, in that same calm and unhurried voice, supplied a detailed description of the attacker and the clothes she had been wearing.

She knew exactly what time the woman had arrived and left the building. Luca could see that she was a sort of witness superstar as far as the police were concerned.

'She thought Alice was my girlfriend,' Roman explained, pulling off the oxygen mask they had fitted to his face. 'She had a knife at Alice's throat and I tried to take it off her.'

'That was very unwise of you, sir,' the policeman observed. To Alice he explained they would need a full statement from her, but the morning would do if she didn't feel up to it tonight.

Somebody else said something about delayed shock and asked if there would be someone at home when she got there. Alice responded to all the questions and showed no signs of breaking down.

Stress! He'd seen people missing a bus display more stress! And Luca couldn't credit that she had actually had a knife held to that lovely throat, though there was a blood-stained nick at the base of her pale, graceful throat that said otherwise!

'Can I come along?' he asked the ambulance crew as they prepared to leave.

'No, Luca.'

'Please, sir, will you keep the mask on?' the sorely tried paramedic asked.

'In a minute…and I really could walk…' The professionals looked amused and Roman didn't push it. 'Luca, you stay. Tell Mum and Dad—I don't want them hearing about this second-hand. Tell them I'm fine.'

'I'll lie through my teeth,' he promised. 'Hang in there.'

'You shouldn't talk, Roman,' his brother's ministering angel quietly cautioned.

'The lady's right, sir. You shouldn't exert yourself,' the paramedic agreed.

Once his brother had been stretchered out Luca slipped into the outer office to ring his parents. He was glad it was his mother who picked up. His father had a volatile temperament and he didn't want to be responsible for him having a second heart attack.

His mother was upset but he managed to soothe her worst fears and promised to ring from the hospital with further news when he got there. He was half out of the door when he remembered the woman in the other room…*actually she wasn't easy to forget*.

He poked his head around the door; the promised forensic team hadn't arrived but everyone else had left. She was alone.

'Can I give you a lift anywhere? I'm on my way to the hospital.'

'The hospital,' she repeated vaguely.

Luca wondered if that delayed shock they had spoken of was setting in.

'Yes.' Her smooth brow creased in concentration as her eyes lifted to his face. 'Yes, that might be a good idea.'

He hovered impatiently at the door, but she made no attempt to follow him. 'I'm going now…if you're ready?'

'Right, I just…the thing is I don't think…'

In the split second before her knees folded he registered that blood that didn't belong to his brother was seeping through the fingers she had pressed to her abdomen.

'I think she must have nicked me,' she roused herself enough to say faintly as he fell on his knees beside her.

'God! Why the hell didn't you say something?'

'Didn't feel a thing.' She winced as he hefted her into his arms. 'Until now. I didn't even know she'd got me. Isn't that amazing?'

He figured if he was fast, he might catch the ambulance before it left. He didn't. There was a solitary uniformed bobby, no more than a kid really, standing beside the pavement that the ambulance had just pulled away from. His eyes widened when he saw Alice.

'Another casualty. Have you got a car?'

The young man shook his head. 'There was no room for me. I'll call an ambulance. I really don't think you should do that, sir,' he said as Luca slid the half-conscious woman in the back seat of his Mercedes.

'Maybe I shouldn't, but we've not got time to debate it. Can you drive?'

The young man nodded.

'Good.' Luca tossed the keys to him. 'Then drive…drive fast,' he added as he slid in the back and put the fair head in his lap.

Just before she lost consciousness she opened her eyes and murmured anxiously, 'Roman will be all right, won't he?'

It transpired that Luca's decision not to wait for an ambulance had been correct. Another few minutes and it could have been too late. Alice had lost part of her damaged liver, but not her spirit—that had remained firmly intact.

Luca was beginning to think that he had not escaped that evening totally unscathed himself.

'The knife thing was instinct or accident or most likely a bit of both. I would have done that for anyone…even *you*!' Alice said. 'Though I'm willing to bet there are a lot of people who would have paid me not to.'

As an image of Luca injured consolidated in her head, so did the bleak empty feeling. A world that didn't have Luca— infuriating, maddening and arrogant Luca—was shockingly unimaginable. But she had lost her husband and loss didn't get worse than that. So why did the idea of losing a man she didn't even like fill her with a dread that lodged like a solid object behind her breastbone?

The feeble voice from that night was now robust and angry, the scared blue eyes now spitting fury. If Luca had been able to think humour when he recalled that night the contrast could have been comical, but it wasn't and he couldn't.

She got to her feet. 'Don't worry, I'm not going to faint this time, but I am going to leave and you're going to pay for a taxi to take me back to the hotel. I think that I deserve a free ride after putting up with your obnoxious company.'

To her surprise Luca didn't put up an argument. He made his farewells to Paolo, who became even more animated when Luca asked for the bill.

'You offend me!' Paolo declared.

'If it hadn't been for Luca here sorting out my accounts there would be no Paolo's.' He took Alice's hand and kissed it. 'And you will bring your lovely lady to see us again very soon.'

Luca's heavy-lidded eyes drifted towards her tense face. 'Very soon,' he promised in a voice that made her stomach flip.

Outside he put her in a cab, unfolded some notes from a wad in his wallet and gave the driver instructions. Without a word he walked away.

Alice was so wrapped up in her own thoughts that it was some time before it occurred to her the journey back to the hotel seemed to be taking an awfully long time.

'Is this the quickest route?' she asked the driver. 'It only took a few minutes to get here on foot.' All she wanted to do was get back to her room, lock the door, and indulge in a bout of unrestrained weeping.

'This is the best way to avoid the roadworks, lady,' he replied and Alice didn't have much choice but to take his word for it. She comforted herself with the reflection that if he was ripping anyone off it was Luca. And to her way of thinking anything that caused Luca O'Hagan a moment's annoyance could only be a good thing.

She closed her eyes and leaned back in her seat. Damn Luca O'Hagan!

The relief she felt when they finally drew up outside the hotel was short-lived. It actually lasted until she stepped out of the glass-fronted lift and saw the tall figure of a man standing down the farthest end of the hallway. The man had sleek dark looks and the sort of inbuilt air of assurance that made him stand out from the crowd. Only there was no crowd, just the two of them.

Alice's heart climbed into her throat. Her firm light step faltered, but she carried on walking. What choice did she have? This couldn't be happening. But it was; there was no mistaking the arrogant angle of Luca's dark head.

As she approached Luca levered himself off the wall. His relaxed manner was a striking contrast to her dry-mouthed discomfort.

'You're not here?' she protested in more hope than anticipation of him vanishing in a puff of smoke. 'It's not possible. I left before you.'

'The impossible is not so very difficult to achieve if you bribe the driver to take the scenic route.'

His casual confession made her stiffen with anger. *'Why?'*

'Because you'd have kicked up a fuss if I'd tried to get in the cab with you.'

'And you *so* hate to draw attention to yourself.'

'You noticed that? Not everyone realises that I'm a shy and unassuming guy at heart.'

Anger flared in her eyes. 'If you came here to be smart, Luca, go away.' She lifted a weary hand to her head. 'Actually go away anyway, Luca.'

'I'm not going anywhere. We've got some unfinished business.'

'You mean you've thought of some other way you can insult me.' She vented a bitter laugh and swallowed, willing the tears she felt stinging her eyelids not to fall. 'Surely not.'

The hard lines of Luca's bronzed face tightened at her sarcasm. 'I think you gave as good as you got,' he retorted. 'But enough of that…you were ill. For all I know you still are, and don't tell me it was having a few drinks that did that.'

'I wasn't about to because, quite frankly, I don't owe you any explanations.' Her defiant eyes collided with his and as their glances locked and lingered an emotional thickness developed in her throat.

'We'll have to agree to disagree on that one,' Luca said regretfully.

Expelling a long sigh, he rubbed a hand along his hard chiselled jaw. There was no trace of the regret he claimed in his face, just sheer bloody-minded determination as, hands thrust into the pockets of his tailored trousers, he sauntered forward.

Alice hardly registered his inflammatory comment. His jacket had swung open and her eyes were glued to his chest…the chest against which she had recently been closely held. Beads of perspiration broke out across her forehead as she recalled the sense of deprivation she had experienced when he had released her.

To walk into his arms…feel them close tight about her, lose herself in that male hardness… There was a rushing sound in her head as she tried to subdue the crazy compulsion to act out those forbidden cravings. *What would he do if she did?*

The concern in Luca's eyes deepened as he followed the flicker of emotion on her face.

'Are you feeling unwell again?'

As she lifted her eyes to his face the shatteringly erotic image of hands—her own hands—moving over the naked, gleaming flesh of his bare chest surfaced from some corner of her subconscious.

'Ill!' She gave a strange, bitter laugh. 'I wish I was. *Stupid*…stupid, stupid!' she gritted before turning stiffly away.

With any luck he'd assume the scornful slur had been directed at him, not herself. How crazy am I? The sexual stuff was bad enough but *this*!

'There's something wrong with you and I think I know what it is.'

Her back stiffened. 'Haven't you got anything better to do than follow me?'

'Probably.'

'I could call Security.' Now that should be interesting. What should she tell them? Take this man away he's making me fall in love with him.

'True, you could.'

Colour heightened, Alice slung him a discouraging look over her shoulder. It didn't discourage.

Hand on her chin, he turned her face up to him. 'You look terrible.'

She flashed him a tight, resentful smile and pulled away. 'I really needed that.'

'I'm just trying to show a bit of concern.'

Alice eased her shoulders against the wall and closed her eyes. '*Concern?* Well, you can see how that would throw me after tonight.'

'Would you have preferred I had said you looked beautiful?' The dark fan of his incredible eyelashes cast a filigree of shadow along his prominent cheekbones as his glance dropped. 'That's so like a woman.'

She bristled angrily at the amused note in his voice. She only just repressed an impulse to tell him that some men found her pretty.

'You lie to women! Surely not?'

His eyes lifted and infuriatingly he looked appreciative of her acid jibe. God, why did he never react the way she expected?

'Are you on some sort of medication?'

'No, I am not on medication!' she retorted indignantly.

'I wasn't accusing you of being a junkie. I meant prescription drugs.' Eyes that were far too penetrating for her liking swept across her face. 'Have you seen a doctor recently?'

'No, I have not seen a doctor.'

One dark brow lifted. 'Will you?'

'Yes,' she hissed from between clenched teeth.

He laughed. 'You're a very bad liar.'

'I'm also very fed up with ridiculous cross-examination. For the last time,' she yelled, 'I am not ill, I'm just…'

He stilled, his vivid eyes narrowing suspiciously. *'Pregnant?'*

There was a palpitating silence.

Alice's small hands clenched into fists at her sides. Of all the extraordinary explanations, Luca had to come up with one that made her look bad. She attempted to treat the accusation calmly. 'No, I am *not* pregnant!'

'Who is the father?' he asked, acting as if she hadn't spoken, which was Luca all over. He wasn't interested in anyone else's opinion…well, not mine anyhow, she thought. This quality might make him a force to be reckoned with in the business world, but when it came to a personal level it made him a total pain!

'Didn't you hear me? Oh, silly me, I forgot, you're far too fond of the sound of your own voice to listen to what anyone else says!'

As someone who broke out in goose-bumps every time she heard that distinctive velvet drawl, she felt pretty uniquely qualified to discuss his voice.

Luca's attention, which had been fixed on his shoes, suddenly switched back to her face. 'It would explain your over-emotional erratic behaviour,' he contended. 'Your hormones are obviously all over the place.'

She exhaled and closed her eyes…wasted breath did not cover this! 'For the last time I am not pregnant!' she repeated, her voice tight with frustration.

His sensual lips twisted in a cynical smile. 'Would you tell me if you were?'

'Only if you happened to be the father.'

CHAPTER SEVEN

SOMETIMES I don't believe the stuff that comes out of my mouth…!

Luca being the father of her baby would require that they had… Inhaling sharply, Alice bit her lip as she was helpless to control the tide of heat that washed over her fair skin.

'That is of course good to know, but as I do not indulge in unprotected sex that would be unlikely.'

'Neither do I!' No sex at all was about the safest you could get! 'And,' she choked, 'you're not going to indulge in any sort of sex with me!'

'Imagine my devastation,' he said drily.

Alice's eyes glowed with dislike as she glared up at him. 'You're the very last man in the world I would have sex with.'

'Which is why you shake every time I touch you.'

Alice didn't even dignify this taunt with a response. 'Let me say this slowly, so that even someone of your limited mental capacity can understand. I am not pregnant. I don't actually carry a medical certificate to that effect concealed about my person—'

'I think it would be physically impossible, given what you're wearing, to actually conceal anything about your person.'

To her horror she felt her body react to his scrutiny. 'Then you'll just have to take my word for it.'

Mortified, she quickly turned away; the darned dress left her precious few secrets, she thought as her nipples pressed stiffly against the silky fabric. The friction created as she moved to open the door was almost painful.

'Permit me.'

'You make it sound as if I have a choice,' she snarled sarcastically as she was forced to stand by and watch him smoothly open the door with the card he had appropriated from her shaking hand.

'So if you're not pregnant, what are you?'

'Very tired...goodnight.'

She was fast, but not fast enough. The door closed, only Luca contrived somehow not to be on the side she wanted him to be when it clicked shut.

He looked around the room. It had no distinguishing features that made it different from any other bedroom in a five-star hotel. 'Nice room.' One brow lifted. 'Nice knickers,' he added admiringly.

Alice took a wrathful gasp and grabbed the pile of clean undies that had been lying on the bed and dropped them into her open case. Straightening up, her face flushed, she closed the lid with her foot.

'What do you think you're doing?'

'I'm still waiting...' he explained with infuriating calm.

She shrugged. 'For some reason you're acting as though I owe you some sort of explanation.' She disguised her discomfort with the fact that he was in her bedroom with a disdainful toss of her head.

'And you don't think you do? I'm the one about to have my face splashed across the tabloids because I came over with a fit of gallantry.'

The reminder made her tummy squirm queasily. 'It's my face too and there's no great secret. I felt slightly faint...' He looked openly sceptical. 'The room was hot and...I had too much wine.' She couldn't tell him the truth.

'I don't believe a word you're saying,' he divulged, folding his arms across his chest.

Alice's frustrated eyes clashed with deep shimmering blue. 'Don't turn your back on me!' she said, catching his arm as he turned towards the phone, which had begun to ring.

A flicker of shock appeared in her eyes as her fingers closed over the expensive fabric of his jacket. If she had been the sort of person who was impressed by a set of iron-hard perfectly developed biceps she would have been *very* impressed; she had felt steel bars with more give than his upper arm.

Luca's brilliant azure eyes travelled from the small shapely hand on his arm to her angry, agitated face. It wasn't until her dazed eyes meshed with his that Alice realised that, not only had she not let go, her fingers were exploring the hard contours of his upper arm.

She gave a shaken gasp and tucked her hands behind her back.

His darkly handsome head tilted slightly to one side as he looked at her. 'Are you going to pick that up?'

Alice blinked like someone waking from a dream, then, mortified, sent him an angry look and moved towards the phone. As she extended her hand it stopped ringing.

'Frustrating.'

Alice ignored the mock sympathy. 'Will you please just leave?' she begged. 'It's late and I have to work in the morning.'

'Ever the efficient assistant,' he mocked. 'As a matter of fact, you could give Roman a message if you see him before me.'

'Of course.' Alice couldn't believe her luck—he was actually going to go.

'Ask him if he knows why I had to carry his assistant out of the dining room.'

A horror-struck expression spread across Alice's face. 'You can't tell Roman what happened!' she protested shrilly. 'You *mustn't* tell him.' It was only when her own eyes automatically followed the direction of his gaze that she realised that in her desire to communicate the urgency of what she was saying she had grabbed hold of his arm again.

She heard herself stupidly mutter, *'Sorry,'* as she rubbed her palms in a circular motion against her legs. The action caused a static build-up that made the dull, satiny fabric cling to the firm lines of her thighs.

'Why must I not tell him?'

'Don't sit there!' she exclaimed in horror as he made himself comfortable on her bed.

He ignored her…*he was good at that.* 'Why must I not tell Roman that you are ill?'

There was no diverting the man once he got his teeth into something.

And if that something was you…your neck…stomach…? Alice felt a rash of prickly heat break out over the exposed sensitive skin of her throat. Maybe he's right, maybe I am ill, she thought. Only a seriously deranged mind could come up with a thought like that.

'I'm not ill. Or,' she added with a grim smile, 'pregnant.' She heaved a heavy sigh. 'I'm…' Her eyes dropped and she shook her head mutely. Opening up about something that was so personal to Luca of all people…she just couldn't do it.

'You're what?' he prompted impatiently.

The crest of dark lashes lifted from her cheeks as she turned her frustrated glare on him and shook her head. 'I'm nothing.'

Something clenched hard in her belly as she watched him uncoil on the bed. She thrilled to the sheer male vitality he projected.

Iridescent eyes sealed to hers, he gave a smile that left his incredible eyes determined. 'You will tell me,' he promised.

'There's nothing to tell.' She pushed her fingers into her hair, unwittingly drawing his attention to the upward tilt of her breasts outlined in the strapless bodice of her evening gown. As the silky blonde threads of hair slipped through her fingers Alice lowered her arms and fixed her unfriendly eyes on his face.

'What are you going to do?' she enquired sarcastically.

'Bring out the thumbscrews? Send me to my room without supper?' Her mocking laugh had a strained sound.

His lashes lifted; the thin line of colour along each cheekbone accentuated the sharp, sculpted contours. 'You're already in your room, and so am I.'

He had mentioned what she had been trying very hard not to think too much about. Alice gulped as her stomach went into a crash dive. Arms crossed over her chest, oblivious to the uplifting effect this had on her full breasts, she rubbed her damp palms nervously over her upper arms. The smooth flesh was covered in goose-bumps.

'Yes, and I've already had my supper, so I don't suppose it was a terribly apt analogy,' she admitted prosaically.

'I find I can usually fit in a midnight snack.'

Alice pretended not to hear the suggestive purr in his voice and responded to his comment at face value. 'I'm sure you can, but is it a good idea?' she asked with a little shake of her head.

'You don't think it is?'

'Well, you know best, but I've heard that after a certain age those midnight snacks have a habit of catching up with men in the waistline department.' She patted her own stomach and looked sympathetic.

'Thanks for the advice,' he said, looking amused as only someone who didn't carry on ounce of surplus flesh could afford to as he placed his hand flat against his washboard-flat belly.

Her eyes followed his complacent action and her pulse rate kicked up several notches.

His voice dropped to a low, disturbingly intimate level as he throatily added, 'You're the big believer in fate. Could be that this is something that is fated.'

Their combative eyes connected and locked, sexual inertia slammed through her body. Alice was nailed to the spot. She had never in her life experienced the sort of blind lust that could literally paralyse; she couldn't even blink. Her mental faculties were equally traumatised.

The last time I saw that colour, she thought, I was lying on my back on the sugary soft sand of a Mediterranean beach. On that occasion she had needed to shade her eyes to cut down the dazzle from the cerulean sky. Luca was advancing inexorably towards her when she rediscovered her power of speech.

'I think you should leave now.' She almost winced to hear the thread of hysteria in her voice.

Luca winced. 'There's no need to yell, woman.' Along with the irritation that gleamed in his eyes there was another, less easily identifiable emotion, something darker, something infinitely more dangerous. It was the other thing that was responsible for the spill of liquid heat low in her belly.

She looked into his beautiful face and her breath snagged painfully in her throat. It frightened her to realise how powerless she was to control her response to him.

Alice felt a sharp flare of panic; Luca knew about women. She could just about live with him realising she was sexually attracted to him...she didn't think she could bear it if he realised that her feelings went deeper...a lot deeper. Pride became very important when you didn't have much else left.

She was going to have to be very careful about what she said and did. 'Ouch!' She hadn't even been aware of backing away until the back of her knee made painful contact with the corner of a table.

'Are you hurt?' His voice was rough with concern as he caught her arm to steady her.

'Like you'd care!' she retorted childishly.

A hissing sound of exasperation escaped from between his clenched teeth. 'Before tonight I always thought you were the most practical person I had ever encountered.'

'Is that why you generally treat me like part of the office furniture?'

'I have never treated you like a piece of furniture.'

'No, you treat furniture better,' she heard herself accuse ridiculously. 'I suppose you prefer women who are decorative, but can't change a plug.'

'The relevance of that statement passes me by,' he admitted. 'Right now I'd settle for boring. *Dio*, woman…you're not fit to let out without a keeper. *Can* you change a plug?'

'Of course I can.' She saw his expression and flushed. 'Don't be ridiculous!'

'*Me* ridiculous? You're the one who picked up the first guy who smiled at you regardless of the fact he could have been a mad axe murderer.'

Alice's eyes grew indignantly round at this gross distortion of the facts. 'Which would have been one up from you! Will you let go of my arm, please!'

With a muttered imprecation he released her. He watched as she rubbed the area.

'Sorry.'

'You should be.'

His response made it obvious her attempt to make him feel guilty was wasted.

'So sue me,' he suggested callously.

Tears sprang to her eyes, her lower lip quivered…she *never* cried. 'I hate you.'

'They do say that hate and love are closely related.'

For a split second she froze, then loosed a peal of caustic laughter. 'In this case *they* would be wrong,' she promised, seeing him through a mist of tears.

'Personally I think hate and lust are much closer related,' he revealed.

Alice's heart started beating like a wild bird in her chest. She bent forward to pick up a cushion that had been knocked to the floor, glad of the opportunity it gave her to school her features.

'If it makes you happier to think I am fighting a base urge to rip off your clothes, go ahead,' she offered, clasping the cushion protectively against her stomach.

'I like it when you talk dirty.'

From somewhere she discovered hidden reserves and didn't react. 'If you think that's dirty you really have led a very sheltered life.'

He gave a wolfish grin. 'I think you know I haven't, Alice, but if you feel you could further my education…?'

'Did I somehow give you the idea I was interested in how many notches you have in your bedpost?' Or that I'd want to be one of them?

'Not up until now, no.'

It wasn't until the cushion fell from her nerveless fingers to her feet that she was aware she had been standing there, for God knew how long, staring at him.

'My God, you really do love yourself, don't you?' she choked.

'I'm a self-sufficient sort of guy.' The mocking light died from his eyes. 'But as much as I like talking about me…'

'You don't,' she inserted, surprise at her discovery reflected in her expression. Despite his celebrity status, what did she actually know about the *real* Luca? Giving a little was what he did to stop people looking any deeper.

'We have that much in common, it would seem, but like they say sometimes it's good to talk and I think you need to…I'm here…'

Alice looked at the hands he held palm up in front of her. After a fractional pause she laid her own hands on top of them.

Now why did I do that?

His long, lean fingers, very brown against her own, tightened as he drew her forward. She must have responded because moments later she found herself sitting on the bed. Luca was on his feet.

'You talk, I'll listen.' When a mulish expression spread across her face he added simply, 'You talk to me or you talk to Roman. The choice is yours.'

Alice took a deep breath and simulated an interest in her shoes. 'I get flashbacks to the…a…attack.'

A stunned silence followed her stuttering admission.

'And that is what occurred earlier?'

She nodded.

'What form do these flashbacks take?' There was no discernible inflection in his voice.

'I don't get them any more...' Her mouth twisted. 'Or I didn't,' she corrected, lifting her head. 'I see the knife...I feel powerless.' She swallowed and closed her eyes. 'But it tends to be muddled,' she added, wrapping her arms tight across her middle as a shudder ran through her body.

'Here.' She looked up surprised as Luca placed a wrap that had been draped over a chair across her hunched bare shoulders. 'I get the feeling you're leaving a lot out.'

The blood, the noise of the ambulance, the hospital smell and the lights in the corridor shining in her eyes and Luca...

'But essentially we're talking a post-traumatic disorder? I have a friend who resigned his army commission because of it,' he added in response to her startled expression.

'Did he, your friend...did he get better?'

Luca studied her upturned features. 'You've never met the guy, but you really care, don't you?'

'Anybody would care.'

Luca shook his head and looked at the top of her fair head. 'Actually, no, they wouldn't. Martin is fully recovered and in his element running an Outward Bound centre for executives who want to bond while building rafts. You said that it had stopped.' She nodded. 'What made it happen again tonight? Was...was it something I did?' he suggested.

'Something you did?' She was genuinely startled by the suggestion. 'No, of course not. It was the perfume,' she explained.

He looked at her blankly.

'Smells can be very evocative,' she told him.

A flicker of something she couldn't identify moved at the back of his dramatic eyes. 'I know.'

She nodded. 'The literature I read explained that things trigger the attacks sometimes…a sound…a word…*smells*. I had some perfume as a present—I started using it just before the first attack.'

His jaw clenched. 'The stalker was wearing it?'

Alice nodded.

'Dio!' he exclaimed, looking shaken.

'It wasn't a very nice perfume really. It was too heavy for me—' she tried to joke.

'Who else knows about this?' he cut in, scanning her face.

She shook her head. 'Nobody.'

Unbelievable! It was unbelievable that she should cope with that alone. Nobody there when the nightmares came. Nobody to share her fears with. Luca decided he must have misunderstood.

'You've coped with this all alone? But your family knew?'

'You have no idea how upset they were when I was in hospital. I couldn't put them through that again.' Her slender shoulders lifted. 'It was my problem.'

His unblinking appraisal began to make Alice feel unaccountably guilty. She tilted her chin.

'All right?' She immediately regretted the belligerent outburst; it made it sound as though she needed his approval for her actions.

A hissing sound of exasperation escaped through his clenched teeth. 'There is self-sufficient and then again there is bloody stubborn. Do I need to say which heading you fall under? If one of your family was in trouble would you want them to lick their wounds alone in a corner? Or would you want them to turn to you for help? Didn't it occur to you that they would be very hurt if they thought you couldn't come to them when you needed support?'

'I don't like a fuss,' she protested weakly.

He rubbed his index finger along the frown line between his brows as though he was trying to figure something out. His eyes narrowed as they focused on her face. 'Alone? You said Roman doesn't know about this?'

'No, and I'd like it to stay that way,' she told him quickly.

Luca shook his head incredulously. '*Madre di Dio*. How is that possible?' he demanded.

'I didn't tell him.'

'Why the hell not?'

The only part of his body moving was the muscle along his jaw, which was pulsing. His stillness had an explosive quality to it.

'Isn't it obvious?' She really couldn't see what he was getting so het up about.

'Not to me.'

'Your brother thinks it's his fault I got hurt in the first place. He feels guilty.' She sighed—from his blank expression it seemed that she was going to have to point out the obvious...Luca wasn't normally slow on the uptake. 'If he knew about this he'd feel simply terrible! You have no idea how he was afterwards; if I'd asked for him to write me a blank cheque he would have.'

Luca unclenched one white-knuckled fist and dragged it through his dark hair. 'So the secrecy is to protect Roman from feeling "simply terrible".'

'He may not show it, but the whole thing was *awful* for him,' she told him reproachfully.

'I hate to be the one to break this to you, Alice, but my brother is not a sensitive little flower. He's a big boy now. But then you've already noticed that, haven't you?'

'I've already told you I don't think of Roman that way,' she retorted primly.

'And do you think of me that way?' Their eyes collided and the raw sexual hunger stamped on his hard, dark features made her mind go blank.

Alice looked at the floor, but she only managed to resist the draw of his earthy masculinity for a matter of seconds before her head lifted. She swallowed to lubricate her vocal cords. 'I try not to think of you at all,' she admitted hoarsely.

'Do you succeed?'

Her face twisted in an anguished mask. 'Luca,' she begged. 'Don't do this.'

'You do think about me, don't you? Maybe as much as I think about you.' His eyes burned into hers and her heart skipped several beats. 'I think about you in your modest skirts and sensible shoes. The silk shirts, do you buy them in bulk?'

'I…I…' The fact that Luca could recite what she wore to work so accurately was another amazing revelation on a night when revelations were the norm. 'You're very observant.'

His lips twisted. 'Yes, aren't I? But you're not wearing your pearls tonight.' An abstracted expression slid across his face as his restless blue glance came to rest on the pulse spot at the base of her throat.

Agonisingly conscious of her own body, Alice lifted her hand in a protective gesture. 'They didn't go with this outfit. They were my grandmother's.' And he really wanted to know this. 'I don't know whether she was right, but she always said you should wear pearls or they lose their sheen.' Her voice faded to a whisper in face of his slow-burning, dangerous smile.

'Their sheen fades into insignificance beside your skin.'

Alice swallowed. 'Don't say things like that.'

He tilted his head to an arrogant angle. 'Why not?'

'If you had an ounce of sensitivity you wouldn't ask and I wouldn't need to tell you.'

Luca's tall loose-limbed frame grew taut. Like a man who had just completed a marathon, he was breathing hard and deep. The rhythmic rise and fall of his chest had a hypnotic quality.

'I may not be sensitive but I think I'd have noticed you've been to hell and back over the last few years if you'd been working for me,' he revealed, grinding one clenched fist into the palm of the other.

Alice, watching him with wide eyes, was acutely conscious at that moment of what a physically powerful man he was. Shaken and excited, she lowered her smoky eyes.

'He must be blind!' The exclamation emerged like a pistol shot.

Eyes fixed on her clasped hands, Alice heard the sound of footsteps as he paced across the room and then back.

'Who?' she asked, bewildered.

'How could he not notice? If tonight was anything to go by it's hardly the sort of thing you can hide.'

'You mean Roman?'

'Who else?'

'Roman doesn't watch me like a hawk waiting for me to do something he can sneer at,' she countered defensively.

'I don't sneer,' he denied immediately.

'Luca, you could give a master class in sneering,' she told him when she had stopped laughing bitterly.

An abstracted expression slid into his eyes as they travelled the length of her body. 'You must be accustomed to being watched.'

'Are you suggesting I'm an attention seeker?'

'I'm saying you're an extremely beautiful woman,' he rebutted in a husky drawl that vibrated through her body.

Heart beating fast, she looked away from the heat in his smouldering eyes. 'Well, Roman did notice something once or twice,' she admitted. 'But I told him it was a migraine.'

'And he swallowed that?'

'There was no reason for him not to.'

'Because you never lie to him.'

His sardonic drawl brought a flush to her cheeks. 'There's no need to be facetious. I suppose *you've* never been economical with the truth.'

His eyes narrowed. 'I'm not sure you could cope with the truth.'

'Try me.'

'Every time I see you wearing one of those provocative silk shirts buttoned up to the neck...I want to...'

'They're not provocative,' she protested.

'They provoke me.'

'I don't button my shirt up to the neck.'

'Don't be pedantic, woman.'

'What do you want, Luca? To call the fashion police and have me arrested?'

'I want to watch you take it off for me. That's what I've always wanted.'

CHAPTER EIGHT

ALICE froze. Every cell in her body just came to a dead stop for the space of several heartbeats. When things began functioning again she started to shake.

'Always…?' She shook her head from side to side in a negative motion.

Luca nodded.

A wispy little sigh emerged from her lips. 'You never said so,' she whispered.

His glittering eyes were filled with self-mockery as they settled hungrily on her face. 'I thought I'd be treading on Roman's toes. Would it have made a difference if I had?' he challenged, scanning her flushed face.

'We'll never know now, will we?'

He sucked in a deep breath. 'We could still find out?' he suggested thickly.

Alice swallowed. 'How?'

Luca held out his hand and she took it. Holding her eyes, he pulled her to her feet.

'Where do we go from here?' she asked.

'Let's play it by ear, shall we, *cara*. Does that suit you?'

She looked directly into the feverish blue glitter of his eyes and swallowed. *Suit me!* The driving desire for him crowded every other thought from her head. Relentless flames of lust licked her body, hardening her nipples to tight, aching buds, melting the secret core of her. Making her ache.

Breathing hard, she caught her lower lip between her teeth. Then she admitted in a throaty whisper, 'Anything you want suits me.'

The blood rushed to Luca's face as a hoarse, incredulous groan escaped through his clenched teeth.

'I want you.'

'Luca…' she moaned.

As he took her face between his big hands his intent was clearly written in the lean, darkly dangerous lines of his face and the suffocating heat in his smouldering eyes.

Her own breathing had become painfully irregular; her hand went in a fluttery motion to her throat to loosen constricting clothing only to find bare skin exposed by the low-cut gown she was wearing.

The movement momentarily diverted Luca, who took hold of her wrist and unpeeled her tightly clenched fingers one by one.

Like petals of a flower.

As Luca touched his warm lips to the centre of her exposed palm his heavy lids lifted, revealing eyes as hot as an Italian summer sky. Alice couldn't tear her eyes away from the mesmeric heat.

She heard a raw half-sob escape from her throat; it was closely followed by a throaty purr of male satisfaction.

He took her hand and laid it against his chest. Alice's eyes widened to their fullest extent as she looked at her own hand, pale by comparison to the dark fingers that imprisoned it.

'This is crazy.' It's my lips moving but whose is that voice? she wondered, hearing the throaty whisper.

Luca's hand fell away but her own stayed in place against his chest. The heat of his hard body was seeping into her stiff fingers; she could feel the slow, steady vibration of his heart-beat through her splayed fingertips.

'Crazy is good,' he told her.

She nodded her head. 'Kiss me, Luca; I'd really like you to kiss me.'

'Tell me you want me first. I want to hear you say you want me.'

Want…! It was possible that she had never wanted anything more in her life than she wanted this! She wanted to know what his lips felt like against her skin; she wanted to know the taste of him, the heat, the hard male strength of him. The depth of her sheer wanting made her head spin.

'Luca, I want you.'

Anticipation made Alice shake; her breath came in a series of short, shallow gasps as she felt his tantalising tongue slide between her parted lips. Her insides turned to warm molten honey as he slowly probed the moist recesses. As the deep, drugged kiss lengthened she stretched upward, her slender back arching as she strove to increase the erotic penetration, and Luca cupped the back of her head with his hand.

When the kiss stopped they remained as they were with his head to one side so that their noses touched, his forehead resting against her own. Alice felt his breath fan the downy skin of her cheeks.

'Bella mia,' he rasped throatily, running his thumb along the swollen curve of her lower lip before tugging the tender skin sensually with his teeth.

Alice gave a fractured gasp. *'Oh, God!'* Her eyes snapped open as he lifted his head. 'Don't stop!' she pleaded in the grip of a raw need that was outside her experience.

'Stop?' he said thickly. *'Cara*, I haven't even started yet.' To back up his claim he curved his hands around her bottom and drew her pliant body hard up against him.

Her eyes widened as she felt the brazen swell of his erection against her belly. He grinned wickedly as she mouthed a breathless, *'Oh…!'*

The grin made him look so incredibly gorgeous that she found the corners of her own mouth lifting.

'I've made you smile at me…a first.'

She tilted her head a little to one side as she trailed her fingers along his sleeve and felt his muscles tense. Love for this incredibly gorgeous man made her heart race as she watched the shift of expression play across the strong planes and intriguing angles of his face.

'Tonight seems to be a night for firsts. Have you any idea how badly I want you?'

'You shall show me,' he promised.

She shuddered with pleasure and closed her eyes as he bent his head and fitted his mouth to hers. The heat in her blood ignited and she was kissing him back with a desperate starved intensity.

The abruptness with which he released her left Alice gasping quite literally and she began to shake with fine tremors that shook her entire body. Her big eyes were fixed with bewildered reproach on his face.

'What's wrong? Did I do something?'

A spasm contorted his lean features. 'You're beautiful.' His eyes slid from hers as he dragged a not-quite-steady hand through his hair. 'You have been drinking…you were ill.' So what's your excuse, Luca?

Alice listened to him with a growing sense of frustrated disbelief.

'I've had a drink; that isn't the same thing as being totally drunk or incapable!' she protested. 'I'm quite able to make my own decisions.' Even really bad ones like kissing Luca O'Hagan.

Dear God, what was I thinking of?

Silly question, I wasn't thinking, I was just acting like a sexually starved idiot!

'Alcohol can affect a person's judgement,' he recited gravely. 'The hospitals are full of young men who made the decision to drive after a skinful.'

'Are you trying to tell me that the consequences of sleeping with you are likely to land me in hospital?'

'You know exactly what I was saying, Alice.' Luca massaged his temples and revolved his athletic shoulders. Neither action released any of the tension that was tying his body in knots.

'I know you won't let a little thing like the facts ruin a good sermon.' She scrubbed angrily at her tear-stained cheeks with her clenched fists and sucked in a tremulous breath. She suddenly buried her face in her hands.

'Tomorrow…'

Her head lifted.

'If you say I'll thank you for this tomorrow I'll kill you!' she warned. 'How dare you tell me I'm being reckless? I'm *never* reckless; I reckon I'm due a bit of reckless. And who would I be hurting? Tell me that.'

'There's no need to act as if you are the only one who's suffering, Alice. This isn't easy for me either,' Luca pointed out with what, when you considered the ache in his groin, was in his opinion admirable restraint.

Pity you hadn't shown some of that restraint five minutes ago, the voice in his head suggested drily.

Was she meant to offer him sympathy? 'Good!' She wanted him to suffer…suffer lots. 'And who says I'm suffering?' she added defiantly.

Consciously controlling his breathing, Luca prized his eyes away from the pouting outline of her full, luscious lips. His mobile mouth twisted as their eyes met.

'My mistake.'

'I can't believe it happened.' Alice wasn't even aware she had voiced her dismay out loud until Luca responded.

'I wouldn't try and figure it out; sexual chemistry doesn't follow a logical pattern.'

Alice studied him with an expression of seething dislike as he moved to the other side of the bed. He couldn't have made it much more obvious he was deliberately putting distance between them.

'Don't worry, I'm not going to jump you!' She felt the hot sting of tears and blinked. She had never felt so mortified in her entire life. 'And for the record there is no chemistry here, sexual or otherwise.'

Luca's expressive shoulders lifted in a shrug that revealed his irritation. He looked at her big tear-filled eyes and quivering lips and his expression softened.

'I'm not drunk, I'm mad! As for you coming down with a case of principles…' she released a hoarse laugh '…just how likely is that?'

Much more likely, she thought, now in full self-pity mode, he had realised whom he was kissing. The incomparable Luca O'Hagan kissing a glorified office dogsbody? That would never do.

'You don't think I have principles?'

'The truth?'

He shrugged. 'Why not? It has a novelty value at least.'

'I think you'd sell your mother for a profit,' she flung back recklessly. 'And…put that down!' she yelled, flinging herself across the room in her haste to snatch the framed photo he was studying out of his hand. She glanced down at the snapshot of Mark and a younger her before glaring at him and clutching it protectively against her heaving bosom.

'Who is he?'

'Mark.'

'*Mark*…my, you do get around, don't you? And where is this *Mark* while you're trying to get me into bed?'

'He's dead.'

The sneer died from his face. 'I'm sorry,' he said abruptly. Electric-blue eyes travelled over the contours of her face, dwelling longest on the softness of her lips still swollen from his kiss. He was very aware of the sweet taste of her mouth still on his tongue. 'He was someone special to you?' he asked thickly.

She nodded mutely. 'Very special; Mark was my husband.'

A look of total astonishment swept across his lean face. 'You were married?'

Alice gave a tight shrug. She didn't want this conversation. Not with Luca, of all people. 'People do get married, you know.'

People, but not Luca, she thought, sliding a covetous look at the tall, lean figure beside her. Luca had never displayed the slightest inclination to settle for one woman. His idea of a long-term relationship was two weeks.

Now that she thought about it, in all but one very important detail he was the sort of man her sister-in-law said she really needed at this point in her life. Alice tried and failed not to recall some of the qualities her blunt sister-in-law had said were essential when looking for a suitable man to make her feel like a woman. 'He's got to be hot in the sack and generous, if you get my meaning?'

It was generally pretty hard *not* to get Rachel's meaning!

At the time an amused Alice had doubted this sex god who could turn your bones to water *and* make you laugh existed outside her sister-in-law's fertile X-rated imagination. Now Alice knew differently! She almost could have been describing Luca.

'So I've heard. When did you get married?'

She replied and he swore softly in Italian. 'Six years ago; you must have been very young.'

'So was Mark.'

Luca narrowed his gaze on her wide, wary eyes. 'How long were you married for?'

Ridiculously the sexy rasp in his voice made her tummy flip. 'Three months.'

His chest lifted as he inhaled deeply in shock. 'Three months!' he repeated. *'Madre di Dio!'* He scanned her averted face. 'Was he ill?' he probed gently.

'Mark got pneumonia, which developed into septicaemia.'

Luca wondered how often she'd been forced to explain these bleak facts, being scrupulously careful not to display any emotion that might embarrass the other person. The Latin and Irish blood running through his veins made him unable to see anything good about the English stiff upper lip. In his view emotions were there to be expressed, not repressed.

The owner of a volatile temperament and strong views, Luca had got into trouble expressing his own in the past. Trouble included losing a job for refusing point-blank to write a juicy story that would have hurt a politician's family, and getting beaten senseless as a thirteen-year-old for telling a group of bullies four years older than him exactly what he thought of them!

Hell, it had to be frustrated lust that was making him see Alice jumping into bed with every man she spoke to…and now he was jealous of some dead guy! His hands clenched into white-knuckled fists as his guts churned with self-contempt.

'He was dead within forty-eight hours.' She connected with his eyes and registered the flash of shock and warmth of sympathy in the startling depths. 'I know, I didn't think that young, fit people died of pneumonia either, not with modern drugs. Well, that's what I thought…' she admitted huskily.

Luca watched her slender shoulders lift; the pragmatic gesture hid a world of hurt. He could only imagine what it must have felt like. The surge of fierce protectiveness that surfaced from somewhere deep inside him froze Luca to the spot; it was one of the strongest, most primal responses he had ever experienced.

'But apparently they do.' For a long time she had been bitter and angry but this had lessened over the years.

'Three months isn't long to get to know your husband.'

'Mark wasn't a complicated person.' Unlike you, she thought. Her husband had been caring and mild-mannered; it was actually hard to think of a man more different from the complex, difficult one who stood beside her. Mark had been a gentle man and theirs had been a gentle love, not a wild, breathless passion, and she had liked it that way. The thought had a defensive quality that made her brow pucker.

'Anyhow,' she added, 'how long does it take to fall in love?' And when did it happen to me?

She was so white he thought for a split second she was going to pass out, then suddenly as she exhaled shakily her cheeks filled with colour.

'You're asking the wrong man.'

'Haven't you ever…?' She bit off her impetuous question and, blushing deeply, she shook her head. 'It's none of my…'

One dark brow slanted sardonically. 'Have I ever been in love? That sort of depends on how you define love, doesn't it?'

'Oh, God, you're not going to give me a body count, are you?'

He saw her grimace of distaste and his eyes darkened with anger. 'Oh, I stopped counting years ago.'

His satiric drawl made her shift uncomfortably but she added defiantly, 'No little black book?'

'In these days of computers? Haven't you heard print is dead?' he asked her ironically. 'Just what the hell have I done to make you think I'm some emotionally shallow bastard?' Before Alice could think about responding to this bitter demand he added abruptly, 'How long did it take for you to fall in love, Alice?'

'Me?' Flustered, she pressed a hand to the base of her throat. She tried to look away but those curiously intense eyes had her held tight. She couldn't even blink. 'I, well…'

'Was it love at first sight?'

'I'd known Mark all my life. He was the boy next door, literally. Well, the farm next door, to be precise.'

'You married your childhood sweetheart?'

To Alice's sensitive ears he sounded disapproving. 'I suppose I did.'

Luca watched through heavy-lidded eyes as she went over to a drawer and opened it. Carefully she slid the framed photo between the layers of clothes inside.

'Do people know you were married?'

Alice repressed the urge to go back and open the drawer. It

was stupid to feel disloyal for closing a drawer. To see anything symbolic in the gesture, she told herself, was just plain crazy. Mark was still part of her life; he always would be. This was Luca's fault. If it weren't for him she wouldn't be feeling this way.

When she swung back to face Luca her expression was borderline belligerent. 'It's hardly a secret.'

'I didn't know.'

'Well, we never exactly reached the cosy-chat stage, did we?' Even *thinking* cosy in the same breath as Luca seemed wildly inappropriate.

'No, we just got straight down to ripping off each other's clothes.'

Alice gasped, her eyes filling with hot tears of humiliation. 'I'm trying to forget.'

Breathing hard, Luca placed his hand palm-flat against the wall and spread his fingers until the sinews stood out in his hand. 'Having any luck?' he asked throatily after an interval of several long, laboured breaths.

'No!' she wailed miserably.

Luca straightened up and, hands linked behind his head, dragged his fingers down his neck, where he began to massage the tight tortured knots of muscles. 'Six years is a long time to be celibate.'

'I'm sure it is to someone who can't go for six minutes without sex!' she flared.

'So you've had lovers?'

'You're unbelievable!' she gasped, staring up at him incredulously. 'Just what makes you think you've got any right to ask me something like that?'

His eyes narrowed on her angry face. 'So you have.'

'Even if I'd had as many lovers as you have, it wouldn't make any difference to what I shared with Mark. Sex is just sex; the love we shared was something else entirely. Mark will always be part of my life.' Her voice thickened. 'And I'll never be alone.' Her eyes flashed as she lifted her chin.

The silence that filled the room after her impassioned declaration seethed with loud emotions.

If Alice hadn't been busy feeling disgusted with herself for using her relationship with Mark like some sort of shield to disguise what she was feeling for Luca, she might have noticed the beads of sweat across his brow and the unhealthy grey tinge to his olive skin.

'That will make your bed crowded for any man who wants to be part of your life now.'

'That's a totally *horrible* thing to say!'

'Sometimes totally horrible things need saying,' he retorted coldly. 'It's very easy to idealise someone when they're dead, especially when you conveniently filter out all the things that irritated you about that person.'

'Well, with you that wouldn't leave much else, would it? Beside a massive ego.' He inclined his dark head sarcastically as though acknowledging a compliment and her lips tightened. 'Mark didn't *irritate* me; he was kind and funny. We didn't fight.'

A nerve beside his wide mobile mouth spasmed. 'Always gave in to you, did he?'

Alice, her hands clenched tightly at her sides, glared at him with loathing. 'You'd like to spoil my memories, wouldn't you?' she accused wildly. 'But you can't. We had a happy marriage, we thought alike, we agreed on almost everything.'

'And that is your formula for a happy marriage?' he questioned incredulously.

'It worked for us.'

His expression was shuttered as his brilliant eyes swept her flushed, impassioned face. 'So you had something you don't expect to recapture and in the meantime you make do with casual lovers.' Ironically, a day earlier that would have made her his ideal woman. At what point tonight had he realised he wanted more from Alice…much more?

'And why *shouldn't* I have lovers?' Alice demanded truculently. 'Not everyone finds me as repellent as you do!'

'Repellent?'

'I'm so glad you find this funny,' she told him witheringly. Actually, as much as she tried not to notice, it was impossible not to recognise he had a quite amazingly attractive laugh even when it was bitter.

'You have no idea, do you?' he said.

Alice flicked a nervous hand through her hair, drawing the end of one curl absently into her mouth. 'No idea about what?' she queried suspiciously.

'No idea that everything you do is…' he raised his expressive hand and prescribed an undulating curve in the air '…*seductive*,' he rasped huskily. 'You have more sex appeal in your little finger, than any woman that ever drew breath,' he announced with the embattled air of a man who had been pushed too far. 'Look, I can't do this now. We'll talk about this.' He shook his head. 'But not now.'

'I don't want to talk. I want to go to bed with you.'

'*Per amor di Dio!*' he groaned, grabbing his thick dark hair in agitated handfuls. 'You are…killing me!'

'That's not what I want to do to you.' She kept changing from hating him, to wanting him!

Luca never knew where he got the strength to get out of that door, but from somewhere he discovered hidden reserves.

Sitting in the cab, because frankly he didn't trust himself behind the wheel of his car, Luca basked in the saintly glow of knowing he'd done the right thing for… Actually, he didn't bask at all! He doubted he had ever felt this lousy in his entire life.

Halfway home he decided that he had proved his point. Alice could be in no doubt now that he had principles. There was no need to push it. If she wanted a casual lover he would be that casual lover. Why not? It was a pride thing, nothing else. His middle name was casual, so why change now? And, he thought, his eyes narrowing grimly, he would make her forget every other lover she had ever had!

'Mate,' he called out to the driver. 'Change of plan—take me back to the hotel.'

The driver was sympathetic. 'Left something behind?'

'Yes, something pretty important.'

The black coffee he had ordered at the desk reached the room just before he did. Luca watched as the young man knocked politely at Alice's door. The door swung inwards and he called tentatively through the gap.

Luca stepped forward. 'I must have left it open. Thanks, I'll take it from here,' he said, pressing a note into the boy's hand.

'Thank you, sir…' His eyes widened as he saw the colour of the note. 'Thank you *very much*. Anything else you want, just call.'

'I think I can manage from here,' Luca returned.

He felt nervous… *This wasn't just any woman; this was Alice.* Alice who from day one had got under his skin like no other woman born.

His footsteps silent on the deep pile of the carpet underfoot, he walked into the room. He could hear the soft sound of weeping before he actually saw the figure hunched in an attitude of abject misery. Alice, her knees drawn up to her chest, was sitting on the bed rocking gently to and fro. Her glorious hair fell in silvery bangs hiding her face from his view, but her distress was obvious.

Automatically Luca took a step towards her. It was then that he saw what was clutched in her hands: the photo of her husband.

He turned and walked away, quietly closing the door behind him. The people he met as he walked through the hotel gave the tall, grim-faced figure a wide berth. Luca was oblivious to the wary looks. It shook him to realise that for a minute there he'd been willing to go to Alice, take her in his arms, make love to her, even though he knew that he would be a substitute. She would close her eyes and think of her husband.

Were fools born or made? It was an interesting question.

What had she said? Sex is just sex. All his adult life that had been true for Luca, but this time sex was not going to assuage the ache in his loins. He wanted Alice to love him…he loved Alice. If he was going to show Alice that it was possible to find true love more than once, he was going to have to stifle his natural inclinations and take things slowly. It might kill him, but he was going to be patient.

After Luca had left her, Alice wept long and hard. Then after the tears stopped she lay on the bed and, shading her puffy eyes against the electric light overhead, did some good, hard, and, it had to be admitted, overdue, heart-searching.

What had Mum said…life had to go on? Something along those lines. Ironic, really—she'd been avoiding living hers all this time because she had never wanted to feel the sort of pain she had experienced when she had lost Mark, and now she had fallen for a man who aroused feelings far stronger than she had thought she was capable of.

When she thought how much Luca could hurt her if she let him it terrified her, but when she thought about never knowing what it felt like to be loved by him it terrified her even more.

She didn't delude herself, she knew a man like Luca would only be interested in a casual relationship. An expression of determination spread across her face. Well, if casual was what he wanted she would show him just how casual she could be, she decided, levering herself into a sitting position.

She looked at the photo in her hand and kissed the smiling image. She accepted that it was illogical to feel she was being disloyal to Mark for falling in love with another man. She would always love Mark, but he was the past and she had to look to the future. Mark had loved life and her and he would be angry if he thought she was using his memory as an excuse not to live life to the full.

With an expression of sad resolve she took the ring on the gold chain and placed it with the photo.

'Time to move on, sweetheart,' she whispered.

CHAPTER NINE

ALICE stood in for the absent Roman at the next morning's meeting. Armed with a confident smile and copies of a comprehensive independent report on the impact of the proposed development on the local flora and fauna, plus attached recommendations to protect the above-mentioned, she took her place at the table.

'I'm deputising for Mr O'Hagan. I hope nobody has a problem with that?'

The spokesperson of the conservation group caught up with her as she was leaving the building. 'Excellent meeting,' he congratulated her.

Alice, professional-looking in her grey tailored suit and silk blouse, smiled as he shook her hand. 'Yes, it did go well, didn't it?'

'Refreshing in this day and age to deal with a developer who doesn't put profit ahead of the environment,' he commended.

Alice stepped into the cab feeling pretty pleased with her morning's work, but by the time she had reached the hotel the warm glow of achievement had cooled considerably. The concerns that she'd managed to push to the back of her mind while she'd been having to field questions, not all friendly, resurfaced.

Or rather *one* resurfaced, the one being what had almost happened the night before. It had been Luca who had called a halt and for some reason that made her frustration a million times worse. Alice knew she *ought* to feel grateful to him for showing restraint.

At least it wasn't lack of interest that had motivated him, she thought with a surge of relief not untinged by complacency. Her skin got hot and her stomach muscles clenched as she recalled the raw hunger in his incredible eyes as he'd looked at her. No man had ever looked at her that way or made her feel so feminine and desired. And no comprehensive independent report ever commissioned was going to cure the gnawing knot of need in the pit of her stomach!

Nothing except showing Luca that his desire was fully reciprocated was going to do that.

He might have guessed, the ironic voice in her head drily suggested.

The previous night now seemed like some erotic dream. Thinking of the frankly wanton things she had done, and said, made Alice get even hotter, and the thing was she couldn't *not* think about them!

How was she going to act when she saw him again? She knew he had a mental image of her trying to rip his clothes off…well, as good as! She was going to seduce Luca O'Hagan; the questions were how and where, as her experience of seducing men was severely limited.

What she needed was to focus. When she needed to think she often swam. Maybe this sort of thinking called for a more extreme form of exercise? She had already used the hotel pool a couple of times that week. Normally Alice had very little interest in breaking the pain barrier, but she knew the hotel also boasted a particularly well-equipped state-of-the-art gym. Perhaps a visit was called for?

After emailing the boss with the results of the meeting she stripped off her working gear and donned a pair of joggers and a tee shirt. Stuffing her swimsuit in a bag, she headed for the hotel spa.

Glancing through the glass wall of the gym at the sweaty bodies and high-tech equipment, Alice grimaced. The atmosphere seemed a bit too testosterone-packed for her and the females who were there were all wearing Lycra that clung to every taut muscle of their beautifully toned, lissom bodies like a second skin. This was the sort of place where you probably had to pass a midriff test before they let you in—tanned and taut only!

Maybe a swim first would be a good compromise; it was excellent aerobic exercise. And she might get inspiration without resorting to lifting weights, getting red in the face on a treadmill and standing out like a sore thumb in her baggy top and joggers.

She was negotiating her way around a lavish arrangement of flowers balanced on a Grecian-urn-type marble display stand when the glass doors of the gym slid open allowing the blast of loud music from inside to spill out into the sitting area. Alice automatically turned her head in the direction of the sound. At that exact second the person she wanted to run into more than anyone else on the planet walked through.

She was only dimly conscious that the two women sipping a herbal tea while earnestly debating the merits of a new wonder cream for cellulite had stopped mid-sentence as the tall figure dressed in a vest and shorts stood framed in the open doorway. A tidal wave of lust and longing washed over her.

'Oh, boy!' Alice heard the soft exclamation but didn't look to see who had made it. She couldn't; her feet were glued to the floor.

Luca, still breathing hard from his workout, had a towel looped casually around his neck. As she watched he dabbed the towel across his face before crumpling the paper cup he was carrying. As he turned he gave a perfunctory smile to the two women sitting there; the smile was still there as his eyes moved past her and then almost immediately back.

The smile vanished.

She saw his chest lift as he inhaled, shock flaring for a split second in his eyes. Then the smile was back, not so impersonal this time and tinged with caution.

It didn't take a genius to figure out why he viewed her presence with caution. He probably thought she was about to take up where she'd left off. Is she going to act as if last night was the start of something deep and meaningful? Alice could almost hear the thought going through his head.

As he came towards her she took a deep restorative breath and smiled. You could say a lot with a smile and body language and she was aiming for something unclingy with hers. If he picked up on 'I really am interested', so much the better.

'Alice.'

You're staring…say something. *Put on some clothes* was not an option, so she settled for a safe, if uninspired, 'You look hot.'

'That's the general idea.'

She tore her eyes from the drop of sweat running down the side of his neck and gave a flustered smile. 'Of course it is.'

'I didn't expect to see you here.'

If it was immediately obvious to him that she didn't work out it was equally obvious to her he did! It was all she could do to keep her eyes on his face. She had never before associated sweaty with sexy but the sheen of perspiration that made his sleek bronzed body gleam made her quiver.

Face the facts, girl, you're incapable of looking at Luca without wanting to touch.

'I thought I might as well make use of the facilities.'

To her immense relief, even though her throat felt dry and achy her voice emerged sounding passably normal. Her arched brows lifted in enquiry. 'Are you staying here?' she added, unable to hide her hope.

'No, I'm not.' His lips twitched faintly as her lips turned down at the corners. 'The building where I live is doing some renovations; our pool and gym are out of action this month. The residents' group have worked out an arrangement with the spa here,' he explained.

'Great.' At least she now had a legitimate reason not to go to the gym for the rest of her stay.

He looked around, brows lifted. 'No Roman?'

Alice shook her head. 'No, he's had to go to Boston for some pet project of his. He flew out last night.'

Luca was acting as if nothing had happened. From his perspective it probably hadn't; nothing that couldn't be dismissed with a shrug anyhow. *Oh, God, did I misread the signals that badly?* she thought.

'Did he miss his meeting this morning? It sounded important when we spoke.'

'I stood in for him.'

'Really!' He sounded surprised.

Her chin lifted. 'You don't think I'm up to it?'

'You obviously are; my brother wouldn't delegate responsibility on account of your blue eyes.' The militant sparkle in the blue eyes in question faded slightly at this conciliatory observation. 'You must admit that it's a lot of responsibility for a secretary to take on.'

'A lot of secretaries have very wide-ranging responsibilities,' she informed him. 'Not all of them get paid for their extra duties.'

'But you do?'

'Very well. I'm well aware of my worth.'

'I'm sure you are.' But presumably oblivious to the youth who had been ogling her through the plate-glass partition all the while they had been talking. Luca casually stepped a little to one side, effectively blocking the young admirer's uninterrupted view of Alice's rear, before enquiring casually, 'So you haven't seen him today, then?'

She shook her head. *If my skin gets any hotter I'm going to end up a greasy puddle on the floor,* she thought, staring fixedly straight ahead.

'Are you feeling better today?'

Her glance lifted. 'If you mean have I been drinking, no.'

He ran a hand through his damp dark hair and fixed her with an exasperated glare. 'That's not what I meant.'

'No?'

'No more flashbacks?'

'What? Oh, no.' She found that she didn't know how to react to the genuine concern evident in his expression. 'I'm sure that was just a one-off.'

'A therapist might be able to put your mind at rest.'

Her jaw hardened at this piece of blatant interference. 'My mind is at rest.'

'Nevertheless it would be sensible to seek professional advice, especially as you quite obviously feel unable to confide in your friends or family,' he observed. 'I've made a few enquiries,' he revealed casually. 'And it seems the best person—'

Alice, her cheeks pink, interrupted. 'I thought you wanted to sleep with me, not offer me therapy, because I should tell you the first interests and the second doesn't.'

After his audible intake of breath there was a charged silence.

Alice took a deep interest in her trainers. If it had been possible to die from sheer toe-curling embarrassment she would be stretched out on the carpet right now. She'd tried for bold; trouble was she'd gone overboard big time.

The warmth in Luca's eyes deepened as he looked down at the top of her head. This woman was born for him—she just didn't know it yet.

'That is good to know and I hope you always feel able to tell me what you want,' he told her in all sincerity. 'Were you just on your way in?'

Alice lifted her head just as he casually gestured towards the gym. Maybe it happened to him so often that he took women telling him they wanted to take him to bed in his stride?

'I changed my mind. I thought I might go for a swim instead.' She pulled her swimsuit from her bag to back up the story.

'Excellent. That's where I'm heading. I'll see you in there. Take care,' he added, touching her arm to prevent her colliding with the two women who were no longer sitting, but were now engaged in some extremely advanced-looking stretches.

Alice had been dimly aware of their exhibition, though unfortunately for them the person the graceful display was aimed at seemed totally oblivious to their contortions.

'No!' she blurted, nursing the arm he had touched against her chest; the brief contact had left her skin tingling in a disturbing way.

In the act of turning away he swung back. 'No…?'

'I can't…can't…' There was nothing more alarming to read in his deep blue eyes than mild enquiry, yet the moment they locked onto hers Alice couldn't string a sentence together.

I look at him and I lose my mind. The things she wanted to say and do to Luca couldn't be said or done in a public place.

'You can't swim.' He nodded in an understanding way.

'Well…I'm…no, I can't.' Why did I say that?

'Are you afraid of the water?'

'No, I just can't swim.' Alice thought guiltily of the medals sitting proudly on her parents' bureau and added in a forced voice, 'That is, I *do* swim, only not very well.'

'Don't worry, I'll teach you.'

Was he serious? 'I really couldn't impose.'

'It's a matter of confidence really,' he told her.

'In that case you must be a very good swimmer.'

He acknowledged her sly jibe with a lopsided grin. 'I'm a very good teacher also.'

'So I've heard.'

He gave his head an admonitory shake. 'You don't want to believe everything you hear, Alice.' Leaving her to wonder about the meaning of his cryptic comment, he sauntered away. As he disappeared around the corner the two women straightened up.

The frustrated glares they gave Alice were hostile.

As she walked away she heard one of them say, 'She's not even slim.'

'God knows,' came the baffled response.

Alice took a couple more steps, then stopped. While she normally didn't engage in debate with ignorant, rude twits, these two hadn't even bothered to lower their voices. With an impish grin and dancing eyes she turned and walked back to them, emphasising the natural sway of her hips.

'I may not be slim but, between you and me, I'm exceptionally good in bed,' she explained.

The sight of their shocked faces and open mouths made her chuckle softly to herself as she walked to the changing room.

Alice slipped into the shallow end of the pool, having first ascertained that Luca was not there yet. Her efforts to break all speed records getting changed had worked.

When he did appear all thoughts of simulating cramp and having to leave the pool were forgotten. She just stared. He was quite simply perfection in motion!

Her eyes darkened and her breath quickened as she watched him with hungry, covetous eyes. There was not an ounce of spare flesh on his magnificent torso, his legs were long, his belly washboard-flat and his shoulders powerful and broad. Her glazed half-closed eyes were drawn to the light dusting of body hair on his olive-toned tanned chest. It narrowed to a directional arrow of dark fuzz on his belly until it disappeared beneath the waistband of the shirts that he wore low across his narrow hips.

The way her nipples suddenly hardened and tingled could have had something to do with the temperature of the water, but the cause seemed more likely to be the image in her head after following that arrow to its source.

She gulped and looked away. Ducking beneath the surface of the water until her lungs burned didn't decrease the raw visceral feelings twisting in her stomach.

A hand like steel suddenly wrapped around her middle. Alice was so surprised to find herself hauled bodily upwards that she took a startled breath. When her head emerged she immediately began to cough. Her head went forward onto the chest of the man who held her as she coughed and spluttered.

A firm hand did some soothing stroking of her bare back as she was convulsed by noisy spasms that racked her entire body.

'What the hell did you think you were doing?' he blazed.

The soothing stops here, she thought. Luca had barely given her time to catch her breath and he was yelling.

'*Me* doing?' she squeaked, seeing his dark irate face through a mist of tears. '*Me?*' she repeated, her voice rising a quivering decibel or two.

'You could have drowned.'

Alice sighed. It was clearly time to fess up. 'No, I really couldn't…' Her voice faded as his incredible eyes darkened and she felt a shudder run through his body.

'Oh, yes, you could. Have you any idea how long you were down there?' Luca had and each second had lasted half a lifetime for him. 'If I hadn't seen you go under have you any idea what could have happened? Then when you didn't come up I…' She saw the muscles in his brown throat work as he swallowed convulsively.

'Why the hell didn't you wait for me to arrive? And where the hell was the lifeguard?' Without waiting for her to respond, he added in a voice that shook with anger, 'It's criminal negligence!'

'I didn't drown, Luca.'

Her quiet words seemed to have a soothing effect on him. 'No. Did you get cramp? Have I said something funny?'

She shook her head and bit her trembling lower lip. 'I didn't have cramp. I was just messing around really.'

'Messing around?'

'Oh, for heaven's sake, if you must know I was fine until you nearly drowned me.'

If she hadn't been busy nearly drowning she would have noticed before now that nothing much more than a drop or two of water separated her lightly clad body from his bare torso.

They were effectively sealed from shoulder to thigh. She was painfully aware of how hard his hair-roughened flanks were against her smoother skin.

She unwound her arms from around his neck and, hands flat against his chest, tried to push herself free but his grip didn't slacken.

'I saved you,' he rebutted grimly.

'My hero,' she intoned with shaky sarcasm.

'I didn't expect gratitude, but…will you keep still or you'll drown us both.'

She gave a scornful snort. 'In five feet of water?'

A muscle along his jaw quivered. 'People have been known to drown in five inches of water. We should get you checked over by a doctor.'

'I'm actually fine. Look at me. Do I look like I'm in need of medical attention?'

Luca accepted her invitation and looked. He loosed his arm from about her waist and, retaining a grip on both her hands, took a step back himself.

Alice noticed that the face so disturbingly close to her own was pale beneath the tan and, though he was looking right at her, there was an odd, unfocused look in his eyes as though he wasn't seeing her.

'I wasn't drowning, you know. I'm actually quite a…competent swimmer,' she admitted guiltily.

'Sure you are.'

His patronising tone made her teeth clench. 'I am.'

'Like I said, it's all about confidence.'

'Perhaps you could tell me what I'm doing wrong?' she suggested innocently.

'All right, then,' he agreed. 'And don't worry, I'm here.'

She secured the goggles that had been hanging loose about her neck across her face. 'Knowing you're here makes me feel so safe.' Then, arms stretched in front of her, she dived cleanly beneath the water. Surfacing a few feet away, she began to swim, settling immediately into the familiar rhythm as her body cut a clean, streamlined swathe through the water.

She reached the far end exhilarated but not out of breath.

She trod water waiting for him to reach her. It didn't take him long; she was technically a better-than-good swimmer but he was much more powerful.

'*Actually*, it's all about timing, technique and breath control.'

'You little witch!' he cried, brushing the water from his eyes with the back of his hand. 'That was your idea of a joke?'

Hair slicked back that way, he reminded her of a sexy seal. 'I tried to tell you,' she reminded him defensively. 'But you were so patronising I couldn't resist.'

'Patronising! I thought you were scared of the water when all the time you swim like an Olympic contender.'

'I'm not *that* good,' she protested modestly. 'The Commonwealths maybe?'

He shook his head, covering everything in the immediate vicinity in a shower of water droplets. 'Damn it, you swam competitively, didn't you?'

Guiltily she nodded. 'It was a long time ago and I'm terribly out of shape these days.'

'You don't look out of shape to me.' His burning glance licked down the full feminine curves of her body attractively displayed in clinging black Lycra.

'Luca…' Her agonised whisper only made him grin.

'Why did you tell me you couldn't swim?'

Without replying Alice lay on her back and with a couple of lazy kicks reached the side where, with a sigh, she flipped over onto her stomach.

'I didn't mean to, it just came out,' she admitted miserably.

Luca, shoulder-deep in the water, curled a hand over the grab rail. 'For any particular reason?'

'Well, you said…and I thought…if you thought then I wouldn't have to swim with you…but…'

'Stop!' he pleaded, holding up his hand. 'You didn't want to swim with me so you lied? Does that about cover it?'

Not meeting his eyes, she nodded.

'Couldn't you have simply just said no?'

Her eyes widened. 'Have you any idea how hard it is to say no to you?' she demanded.

'Do you find my company so distasteful, Alice?'

'*I wish!*' she exclaimed unthinkingly.

'Then you like my company?'

'Oh, for God's sake, Luca, don't you understand? I can't string two words together when you're fully dressed,' she revealed incautiously. 'I *knew* I'd do or say something really daft if I saw you like…' Her eyes met his and she groaned before sinking once more beneath the surface.

Alice opened her eyes and found herself looking into Luca's lean dark features. Her lips parted in a startled 'O' of shock.

As she kicked for the surface Luca grabbed her shoulders, his mouth sealed tight to hers preventing the bubbling air escaping. Alice twisted her arms tight around his neck and wound her long legs around his hips. Tightly entwined that way they slowly rose upwards.

As their heads broke the surface they both reacted simultaneously, gasping hungrily for air.

Luca, his chest still heaving with the effort to replenish his oxygen-starved lungs, was the first to recover.

'That gives an entirely new meaning to mouth to mouth.' His eyes slid to her full lips and lingered on the lush pink softness. 'You know, you have the most indecently seductive mouth I have ever seen,' he imparted throatily.

Without a word Alice took his water-drenched face between her hands and lovingly stroked the dark hair from his face before pressing her lips hungrily against his.

'You are so beautiful it makes me want to weep,' she confessed against his mouth. 'I simply can't bear it…I…' She broke off as his hands curved around her buttocks, drawing her body towards his.

Luca's eyes dwelt on the vulnerable, exposed length of her slender neck. He sucked in a deep, painful breath before pressing his mouth to the base of her throat. Slowly he worked his way lovingly upwards until he reached her lips.

They kissed, both driven by the same unspoken desperation, deep, drowning kisses that made Alice's vision blur and her heart ache.

The pool attendant cleared his throat for the third time before the couple noticed he was there.

'Is there anything I can do for you?'

Luca responded to such exquisite tact with an appreciative smile. 'Actually we were just leaving.'

The young man looked relieved.

Alice slid her fingers into the wet hair at his nape and touched her thumbs to the strong angle of his jaw. She gave a discontented pout. *'We are?'*

'He was tactful, but that poor guy was basically saying *get a room*. Didn't you hear that?'

Alice shook her head from side to side. 'I was distracted,' she admitted.

Luca's tongue darted out to touch the finger she ran across his lips. 'You're distracting. But about that room?'

'I have a room,' she recalled happily.

'So you have. Do you think it might be a good idea to continue…this there?'

'Anywhere you like.' And shockingly she meant it. If Luca had wanted to make love to her there and then she would have had no objections.

'Right then, perhaps?' He extended a hand.

Alice ignored his hand and, palms flat on the Italian-tiled poolside, levered herself out with an agile twisting motion that left her seated on the poolside with her toes dangling in the water. Aware that Luca's eyes were closely following everything she did, she gathered her long hair in one wet hank over one shoulder and twisted until the excess moisture dripped onto the floor.

'You've done that before.'

Alice gave her head a flick that sent her hair flying backwards. 'It's a matter of confidence,' she confided, smiling.

'Witch,' he accused huskily. Then as his eyes slid over her voluptuous dripping form he corrected himself. 'No, mermaid.'

She held out her hands to him. 'Aren't you getting out?'

'I think it might be better for all concerned if I waited until I cooled off.' In response to her baffled frown his eyes dropped significantly.

'Oh!' she gasped, scrabbling to her feet. 'I see.'

'You, I don't mind seeing,' he admitted. 'Maybe I'll do a few lengths?'

'Excellent idea, I'll see…that is, I'll…later.' As she headed for the women's changing room she heard the sound of his husky laughter.

CHAPTER TEN

'ARE you going up?' Luca asked from within the lift.

The elderly couple who reached the lift before Alice nodded to Luca. 'Very kind,' the woman murmured as he stepped aside to let them enter.

'And, Alice!' He affected shock as he saw her approach. 'Now this is just spooky. I was only thinking about you…well, not five minutes ago. How are you?'

'Fine.'

'You look marvellous.' He appealed to the couple already established in the lift. 'Can we fit another little one in?'

'Of course.'

She squeezed past him into a corner to mutter with a pleasant smile fixed firmly on her face, 'If you don't shut up I'll kill you.'

In her experience awkward silences were the norm for lifts, but the short one that followed her gagging order had a life of its own! His whistling didn't help either. For the benefit of their interested audience and her nerves she made a valiant attempt to initiate a normal conversation.

'I understand you're renovating a place in Tuscany, Luca,' she said in a bright, slightly too loud voice.

His eyes flickered in her direction. 'Yes.'

Her teeth grated as he started whistling again. 'And Roman

says your family have owned property in that valley for generations. He says it's very beautiful.'

Luca scanned her frustrated face. 'Are we going to have a conversation about property?'

'That's the sort of thing people talk about in lifts,' she whispered.

The lift stopped and the couple got out but three more people got in.

'Roman's right, it is very beautiful, but if you're angling for an invite I'm afraid—'

The first sniff of rejection and her defences sprang into life. '*Me* angle for an invite from *you*!' She injected a double dose of scorn into her laughter. 'I don't get many holidays and when I do I like to spend them with like-minded people whose company I enjoy. People,' she added pointedly, 'I can relax around.'

One dark brow lifted. His eloquent eyes sparkled with malicious mockery as they skimmed her flushed, antagonistic face. 'You can't relax around me?' His glance dropped to her tightly clenched hands. 'I can see we'll have to put some work in on the relaxation front. But actually,' he continued, 'I was about to explain that the facilities are primitive as yet.'

'*Oh!*'

'Actually the facilities are non-existent,' Luca admitted. 'No running water, no electricity—'

'You've had problems with your contractors?' It was some comfort to know that things didn't always go Luca's way. He had problems with tradesmen like normal people.

'No, I'm doing most of the work myself.'

Her eyes grew round with astonishment as they focused back on his face. '*You!*'

His wide, sensual mouth curved into an amused smile that widened to reveal a set of perfectly blindingly white teeth.

Attractive smile, she immediately registered.

'It must be the peasant in me.'

Alice blinked to clear the distracting image that immediately entered her head of Luca stripped to the waist revealing tautly muscled golden flesh glowing with the honest sweat of labour. She swallowed convulsively and, aware of their audience, arranged her features into an expression of bland interest.

'Sorry, I'm boring you.'

Too bland.

'No, actually, I am interested. My sister is a furniture restorer…on a small scale. She and her husband renovated an old granary and she said that finding craftsmen who could recreate the original artisan's work was the hardest part of it.'

Luca nodded. 'That's true, but it's not why I'm doing the work myself. I get a kick out of building with stone.' He narrowed his eyes as though he could see the stone he spoke of and made a descriptive fluid gesture with one hand.

Her eyes were drawn to the long, tapering length of his brown, infinitely elegant fingers. A shiver traced the tingling path of the imaginary caress that travelled the length of her spine and was followed by a second wave of heat that left her fair skin washed with rosy colour.

The lift stopped yet again, disgorging and taking on passengers. Did nobody take the stairs any more? Carrying on a normal conversation when her entire body was tingling with arousal, when her head was filled with erotic images, was not easy.

'Roman says it will be quite a show place when it's finished.'

'It's a long-term project but sometimes things are worth waiting for, don't you think?'

No longer caring about keeping up appearances, she gave a deep sigh. Just looking at him made her ache with longing. 'If I have to wait much longer…I'll…'

Luca pressed a finger to her lips. 'Keep it together, *cara*,' he whispered into her ear. 'We're nearly there.'

To see this incredibly beautiful woman almost fainting with lust for him was one of the most arousing experiences of his life…second only to the underwater kiss. The next project in Tuscany would be a very large pool.

When the lift finally reached her floor Alice all but fell out in her haste to escape.

'Do you and my brother have a lot of conversations about me?'

She blinked as her eyes connected with his blissfully blue eyes. *Blissful blue?* Oh, God, this is just what I need! Why is it we women insist on falling in love with and weaving our sexual fantasies around the most unsuitable men we can find? she wondered. Her attempt to trivialise what she was feeling didn't help. She wanted Luca with every fibre of her being and she loved him with an equal intensity.

'You're hardly out of our thoughts.' The truth, even though she hadn't admitted it to herself before, was that once she'd realised that she was milking her boss for information about his brother she had made it a rule not to mention him at all.

Sexual fantasy was fine, she reminded herself. But that was not what this was; this was real. Was she ready for real?

'That might have been the longest few minutes I have ever spent,' he said. 'All I wanted to do was kiss you senseless. Have you ever made love in a lift?'

She swallowed and asked hoarsely, 'No, have you?'

'The things I haven't done could fill a book, but it wouldn't be as thick as the book filled with the things I've imagined doing to you.' Luca watched her lips part in a soundless sigh and he lowered his head.

The depth of her response shocked Alice and, from the look in his eyes when he lifted his head, she thought maybe it had shocked Luca too.

He ran a hand over her still-damp hair, trailing his fingers in the soft, fine ringlets around her face. 'You're incredible,' he said, short of breath.

'So are you.' He reached for her but she stepped back,

shaking her head. 'Come on, we'd better go to my room or we could get arrested. Now that would make the headlines.'

'You could be right. My sense of decorum goes out of the window when I'm around you.'

Approaching the door, Alice turned her head. 'About the headlines... Our photo wasn't news, after all.'

'No.'

Something in his voice made her query. 'Do you know something about that?'

'I called in a few favours,' he admitted, stepping through the door behind her.

Alice gulped when she heard it click closed, but didn't turn around.

'Alone at last.'

She felt him walk up behind her, she felt the long, lean, hard length of him up against her, and with a purr that was part sheer relief she leaned into him.

Luca leaned down and pushed her hair back. 'I love the way you smell.' Her head fell back against his shoulder as he kissed her neck.

'I like that.'

'We like the same things,' he rasped huskily. 'Do you like this too, *cara*?'

Alice gasped as his big hands came up to curve possessively over her incredibly sensitised breasts. Unable to speak, she nodded. Her eyes closed as his fingers slid down the loose neck of her top caressing the smooth upper slopes. With unerring accuracy he located the front fastening catch. She gave a stifled moan as his fingers moved over her aching flesh.

Her spine arched when he located her nipples. She lay there passively while ripple after ripple of hot sensation swept through her as he teased the rosy peaks. When she could bear his clever caresses no longer she twisted around and wrapped her arms around his neck.

Luca's eyes burned with a dark fire that made her quiver

with anticipation as he caught her wrists and held them above her head. Then, still looking into her hot, aroused face, he took the hem of her top and pulled it over her blonde curls. Very carefully he pushed the lacy fabric of her loosened bra back to expose the full proud swell of her breasts.

His fierce gasp was audible. 'You're incredible! Perfect.'

Alice gasped his name out loud as he dropped to his knees in front of her. Her teeth were chattering helplessly with reaction to what was happening. 'What are you doing?'

In reply he placed one hand in the small of her bare back. The lightest application of pressure brought her towards him. The first brush of his tongue over one erect rosy nipple and she was lost. The contact sent a surge of pleasure like nothing she had ever known through her body.

'My God!' Her entire body shuddered in reaction. She knew the erotic image of him kneeling there before her would never leave her.

'You like that?' he asked in a whisper.

In reply Alice slid her fingers into his lush dark hair and shut her eyes tight as he went exactly where she guided him. The sensual touch of his hands and mouth made her skin burn with desire until her skin felt as though she were literally on fire. Her entire body was so sensitive to his touch that the lightest caress made her squirm and moan.

When his fingers slid under the waistband of her trousers, skating lightly over the soft curve of her belly, the feral moan lodged in her throat escaped in a long, low, keening cry.

Luca's head finally lifted. The strain he was under was etched in the tenseness of his features and the blazing heat of his darkened eyes.

She ran her fingers down the curve of his cheek. 'Please, Luca.'

His lips curved in a slow, sensual smile, then without saying a word he rose in one fluid motion and almost casually lifted her into his arms.

He lowered her on the bed, carefully pausing to smooth her

hair around her face. Kneeling over her, he ran his tongue over her quivering lips before plunging deep inside her mouth… again and again.

Her hands slid off his shoulders as he levered himself away from her and Alice opened her eyes. In the grip of wild and uncontrollable emotions she cried out. 'I love your mouth…'

'That,' he said thickly, 'makes me happy.'

Eyes half closed, she ran a finger along the swollen outline of her own full lips. 'Good, I want to make you happy.' *Because I love you.*

He didn't respond to this husky confidence, but the hands that were sliding her trousers down her legs developed a tremor.

Moments later she was completely naked.

'You're beautiful.' The primitive need stamped on his features made the breath catch in her throat.

'Even with this?' She moved her hand to cover the ugly scar faded now to a thin white line on her abdomen.

'What are you—?' she cried out in startled confusion as both her hands were imprisoned either side of her head. Luca's big body curled over her. His eyes blazed angrily down at her.

'Never try to hide yourself from me, Alice.'

She felt overwhelmed and excited by this masterful display. 'I won't.'

He scanned her face, then, apparently satisfied with what he saw, grinned. 'I feel pretty overdressed.'

She watched—how could she not?—her heart beating fast as he fought his way out of his clothes with flattering urgency and a total lack of self-consciousness.

He was every bit as breathtakingly magnificent as she had imagined. A flush ran over her skin as she lowered her eyes and swallowed; he was very aroused.

The mattress gave as Luca joined her on the bed. He laid his hand on the curve of her hip as he stretched out beside her until they lay thigh to thigh.

Alice turned her body towards him as she laid a tentative

hand on his flank. She was shaking. 'I've wanted to touch you for such a long time.'

A sigh shuddered through Luca's body and she felt the vibration through her fingertips.

'Then touch me, *cara*,' he rasped, kissing the side of her mouth.

Alice accepted his invitation until his painfully aroused body could bear no more. He slid his hands between her smooth thighs. A keening cry of pleasure left her throat as his exploration deepened.

'Is that for me…?' he asked thickly as his fingers slid into her moistness. She shook her head mutely and pushed against his hand, moaning.

'You're so tight…so hot…'

'Oh, God…Luca…' she cried, her face twisted in anguish. 'Please…'

Luca's eyes were fixed on her face as he slid between her thighs and entered her in one smooth upward motion into the slick heat.

'You're so…so…I…' she cried brokenly, almost sobbing as she felt him fill her. When he began to stroke inside her she lost all sense of anything but the man who possessed her and the pleasure that stretched her senses to the utmost limit.

Her hands curved over the firm contours of his tight buttocks and her legs locked tight about his waist as he began to move faster and harder. Finally, when she thought she could bear no more, her body was convulsed by a shatteringly sweet climax at almost the exact moment she heard Luca cry out and felt his body shudder.

CHAPTER ELEVEN

LUCA considered time his most important commodity; he didn't participate in endless meetings where pieces of paper were pushed around the table and no decisions made. He had no problem with people who disagreed with him; in fact he encouraged a lively exchange of views. One of his pet hates were people who sat on the fence.

This afternoon's meeting had by his own criteria been a total waste of time and the only person he could blame was himself! He had been totally unable to focus on the problem in hand...not only that but he didn't care!

His ability to ruthlessly compartmentalise his life had deserted him with a vengeance. Physically he had been in the meeting but in every other way he had been elsewhere...no prizes for guessing where!

Leaving a warm bed and the arms of an even warmer woman had required every ounce of his not-inconsiderable will-power. Alice had simply looked mildly surprised when he had suggested cancelling his meeting.

'Don't be silly, Luca. You wouldn't expect me to cancel a meeting for you, would you?' she'd reproached, stroking his cheek.

Yes, I damned well would!

He'd stopped himself saying it, but only just. How could she treat what had passed between them as a casual coupling?

The supreme irony of his outraged thought suddenly struck him forcibly. He threw back his head and laughed out loud, a grim, harsh sound that made a nervous temp walking by stare at him.

Luca O'Hagan, the man who was a renowned commitment-phobic, was feeling badly done to because a woman had not acted as though her world would come to an end if he didn't call back. Actually from the way she'd acted it was difficult to imagine her losing an hour's sleep if he vanished off the face of the earth!

A taste of your own medicine, O'Hagan?

Alice had been his dream lover made flesh and blood in bed—warm, soft flesh, giving, warm and wild. Out of bed? Well, if she hadn't shown him the door, she hadn't seemed too damned bothered when he had gone through it! His jaw clenched as he recalled her response to his suggestion he ring her later.

'That would be very nice, Luca, but don't worry if you can't,' she had told him with an absent smile that had suggested her thoughts had already been elsewhere.

Nice!

Luca had swallowed his anger and salvaged a little pride simulating the indifference Alice was displaying.

'Well, actually I've got a full day.'

Had the flicker of hurt he'd seen in her eyes been wishful thinking? Certainly her practical shrug and cheerful smile had not suggested she would be hanging around waiting for him to call. Deciding he could wait until she realised she needed a flesh-and-blood man, not a dead hero, was fine in theory; in reality he frankly didn't think he could handle it.

One of the joys of being the boss was when you decided to take a walk in the park…*literally*…nobody was going to say a word. The fresh air might clear his head. It sure as hell needed clearing.

He reached the park and it began to rain, which made him think of home—Ireland. Luca, who considered himself cosmopolitan, a city boy through and through, experienced an unaccustomed pang of homesickness for the green isle of his youth.

By the time he sat down on a bench the sun had come back out. He brushed some of the excess moisture from his hair with a careless sweep of his hand as he stared into the distance, an abstracted expression on his handsome face. A couple walked by oblivious to the rain. Looking at their linked hands made his chest tighten. What the hell is happening to me? he thought.

Whatever it was he had to share what he was feeling…and that was definitely a first!

When he got back he cancelled his appointments for the rest of the day and caught a cab to the hotel. The manager saw him crossing the lobby.

'I'm afraid your brother isn't here at the moment, Mr O'Hagan.'

'Pity.'

'I understand he won't be back until the morning.'

'Has Miss Trevelyan gone with him?'

'No, I believe the young lady is still here. Shall I have them ring her and say you're on your way up?'

'Don't bother, I'll surprise her.'

There was a purposeful spring in his step as he approached the door. He went to knock when a maid carrying linen let herself out of the room. Luca nodded and stepped into the room past her. His lean body tensed as he heard the sound of Alice's voice; she was obviously on the phone.

He was in the act of revealing himself when he registered what she was saying. The blood drained from his face.

'Yes, pregnancy test…that's right. Sure I'll hold…'

Luca could hear her humming softly under her breath as she waited. He raised a hand to his temple and massaged the spot where a vein visibly pulsed beneath the golden sheen of his skin.

'And there's no doubt it's definitely positive… Right, thank you very much.' Alice, punching in her sister-in-law's number, didn't see the tall figure who slipped silently from the room.

The phone was picked up immediately. 'It's positive—you're going to be a mum.' Alice couldn't stop grinning. 'The nurse at the doctor's sent her congrats and said you should ring for an appointment to see her and the doctor. I explained you were going back to England tomorrow.'

'I'm going to have a baby…' The sound of soft sobs echoed down the line.

The shock and wonder in the older woman's voice made Alice's own eyes fill up. *Relax* had been the doctor's advice to her brother and his wife when all the tests had given them both a clean bill of health. That had been ten years ago; no wonder her sister-in-law sounded gobsmacked.

'You're *sure* they said it was positive?' Rachel hesitantly asked after a lot more sniffing.

'Totally sure.' Alice wasn't surprised that Rachel sounded as though she couldn't believe it. After three false alarms her distrust was hardly surprising.

'Oh, God, I don't know what I'd have done if you hadn't been over here,' admitted Rachel, who was on a visit to her parents in Long Island. 'I couldn't tell Mom until I was sure—not after last time.'

Alice gave a sympathetic murmur. The 'last time', by the time Rachel had realised the home pregnancy kit was not as foolproof as it claimed, she had given half her friends and family the glad tidings. She had then had the horrid task of telling them she wasn't pregnant after all.

'I know you must have thought I was crazy when I asked you to phone the doctor's office, but after all the other times I was just *so* nervous. Oh, God, what will Ian say? Why isn't he here?' she added in the next breath. 'That would make everything perfect.'

'Well, he's due home next week, isn't he?' Alice comforted the wistful mother-to-be.

'Tuesday morning.'

'How long since you saw him?' Alice had boundless admiration for her sister-in-law, who coped stoically with her husband's long absences.

She wasn't sure she would have coped as well as Rachel if she had been married to a navy officer. His own wedding was about the only family occasion her brother had made it to in the last ten years!

'Three months. What's the betting he won't be around for the birth?'

'I'm sure he'll try to be.'

'Well, if he's not…I hope you don't mind me asking this, Alice, but would you mind being there as my birthing partner? Well, actually, I'd like you to be there even if Ian is there. You know how bossy he gets—he'll probably put up the backs of everyone at the hospital.'

This unexpected request made Alice's eyes fill with emotional tears again. 'Are you sure it's me you want?' she queried, incredibly touched to be asked.

'There's absolutely nobody I'd prefer,' Rachel replied firmly.

'If you want me I'll be there. I don't know that I'll be much use,' Alice warned. 'But I'll be there with bells on if you want me,' she promised eagerly. She privately resolved to read up everything she could on the subject.

'Always supposing that sexy boss of yours can spare you.'

'Roman? If I added up all the overtime I've put in for that man he owes me a *year's* holiday.' Alice frowned when there was no response. 'Rachel…Rachel…?'

'Sorry,' came the breathless reply seconds later. 'I was just dancing around the table.' Her voice dropped to an awed whisper. 'God, Alice, I'm going to have a baby! Isn't it incredible?'

'Absolutely,' Alice agreed fondly.

'What were you saying?'

'Nothing, I just said leave the boss to me,' she recapped quickly. 'When is the great day? Have you worked out when you're due?' Rachel told her and her eyes widened as she made a quick mental calculation. 'That makes you almost four months gone!' she exclaimed.

'I know. Ironic, isn't it? I spend years getting excited if I'm half an hour late and when I actually fall pregnant…' she gave a burble of euphoric laughter '…I don't even realise it until I'm almost four months! And if Mom hadn't remarked on how much weight I'd put on I'd probably still think I had indigestion.'

'What are you going to call indigestion? Do you want a boy or a girl? Gosh, what if it's twins?'

The two women spent a happy half-hour talking baby names and somehow, Alice wasn't sure how, but as often happened when two women chatted, they got onto the subject of men.

Alice thought she was being incredibly discreet until Rachel said, 'Does he have a name, this man we're talking about?'

'I was talking hypothetically.' She was glad that her sister-in-law couldn't see that she had gone the same colour as her freshly painted toenails—scarlet had seemed appropriate under the circumstances. 'You didn't think I was talking about me?' Sometimes she forgot that Rachel actually *listened* and in doing so often heard the things you *weren't* saying.

'Sure you weren't.'

'I wasn't!'

'It sounds to me like you're pretty smitten.'

'Good God, no, it was just casual.' *For him at least*, and she had tried, she had really tried, to follow his lead even though she had wanted to lock the door and tell him he couldn't possibly leave.

It was irrational, she knew, to feel bitter. It wasn't as if he had offered her anything but sex. She ought to be grateful that he hadn't lied to her the way some men did. At least this way they both knew where they stood.

At least she hadn't done anything terminally stupid such as tell him of her undying love! When she recalled how close she'd come her blood ran cold.

'Then we are talking about you.' Rachel sounded smug. 'I thought so. About time too,' she approved. 'Now tell me all—who is the lucky guy? Is he incredibly gorgeous?'

'I don't even like him,' she lied.

'So it's pure animal lust. Well, that can be fun too.'

Alice had no intention of discussing animal lust with her embarrassingly outspoken sister-in-law. 'Great fun,' Alice agreed unhappily.

'Is there a problem?'

'No problem, we just…we don't actually have much in common.'

'So this isn't a meeting of minds. Does that matter if the sex is great? It's not like you're planning to marry the guy, is it? Like I keep saying to Ian, Alice got married so young, she never really let down her hair and did the crazy, irresponsible, single-girl bit.'

Alice's lips quivered as she imagined how her protective big brother would have reacted to the opinion his little sister should be crazy and irresponsible.

'You need to test-drive a few men, compare and contrast. You know what I mean?'

'I get your drift, Rachel.' The sparkle of humour died from her eyes as an image of Luca came into her head. Luca with his incredible eyes sparkling with sexual challenge, his sensual lips curved into an insolent smile. Compare and contrast? Luca was quite simply incomparable!

The only way to go after Luca was definitely down. Though down might be less exhausting, both emotionally and physically, than Luca.

'The sex *is* great, I take it?'

Alice blinked. Eyes half closed, she recalled the way her treacherous body had responded to Luca's touch, his raw masculinity. Even thinking about his voice made her tummy muscles clench.

'*I* thought it was.'

The sound of Rachel's exasperated sigh echoed down the line. 'Sometimes British self-deprecation is kind of sweet, other times it's just plain irritating! Who is this guy, anyway? Have you known him long?'

'I've known him but we haven't…that is, Lu…he…we…'

'Good God, Alice, you're not talking about Luca O'Hagan, are you?'

'I might be…' There was a definite edge of defiance in Alice's response.

'Luca O'Hagan. My God. He's a total stud, but, no offence, isn't he a bit *deep end* for someone like you?'

Alice appreciated her tact, but she needn't have bothered. She was perfectly aware that the likes of Luca wouldn't normally look twice at someone like herself. But he had looked, and more, hadn't he? And furthermore he'd acted as if he enjoyed looking.

'Alice, be careful won't you?' she heard Rachel say worriedly as she tuned back into the conversation.

It could be too late for that, Alice admitted as she forced herself to concentrate on what Rachel was saying.

'I'd hate to see you get hurt. His reputation—'

'I know all about Luca's reputation, and, don't worry, I can take care of myself. It's not likely it's going to happen again.'

'Do you mean that?'

'Of course I mean it.' I mean it right up to the moment he walks through that door. If, she thought bitterly, he can drag himself away from his meeting. She could almost see his tall, athletic figure, framed in the doorway.

'You sound as if you're sorry about that.' Alice blinked away the imaginary Luca and her sister-in-law continued. 'Was he *that* good?'

'*Rachel!*'

A wicked-sounding chuckle echoed down the line. 'My husband's been at sea for three months. The only sex I have is vicarious,' she excused herself.

Despite herself, Alice grinned. 'Let me put it this way: chocolate is good, but you'd get bored if you had it for every meal.' Wasn't chocolate addictive?

'That good, huh?' came the impressed response.

No wonder Rachel had been so shocked, Alice thought as she stood under the hot needles of the power-shower spray. Me and Luca—what am I thinking of falling for a man who changes his women the same way most men change socks?

Be careful, Rachel had said, and she doubted her sister-in-law had been talking birth control when she had said that! No doubt she assumed that when you were talking to a twenty-eight-year-old, well-educated female who ought to know better this wasn't the sort of thing that needed discussing!

Luca had probably thought the same thing. No doubt he had taken it for granted that she had taken precautions. Though given his claim to never have unprotected sex it did strike her as slightly unexpected that he hadn't done something about it himself. Of course the chances were…what…even given her erratic cycle…*minimal*…?

I can't think about that now!

She had to focus her thoughts and energy on the things that she *could* control…like being good at her job and not acting like a total idiot when she saw Luca again. If they were going to have a sexual relationship she would have to accept some very brutal truths and keep some very difficult secrets. She had serious doubts when it came to her ability to disguise the depth of her true feelings.

She selected a pair of jeans that made her hips look relatively slim—her bottom might be generous but at least it was firm—and topped it with a white designer tee shirt and tailored jacket. She had some free time and if her credit-card limit was not going to allow her to literally shop until she dropped she was hoping that the retail therapy would still be therapeutic. If she didn't think about Luca for half an hour it would be worth the expense!

After a final check of her reflection in the mirror she stepped out into the corridor where she almost walked into someone standing outside the door. She raised her hands to stop herself colliding with the stationary figure.

'Sorry.' She lifted her head and the breath rushed out of her lungs in one sibilant sigh as she found herself looking up into a pair of electric-blue eyes. 'Luca…you here… now…how?' She bit down hard on her lip. Me Jane, you Tarzan would have been a step up from that disjointed gibberish.

Start again. From somewhere she dredged something that passed for self-possession.

'Luca…' Good tone, casual and relaxed, but not too relaxed. It gave no hint of the tumultuous state of her pulse or the mortifying condition of her nervous system, which was what counted.

'You remembered my name, I'm touched.'

Alice was too occupied repressing her basic instincts to pick up on any undertones beyond casual sarcasm in his comment or his strained attitude.

'What are you doing here? I was just on my way out.'

His dark brooding features hardened perceptibly. 'Then you can change your plans.'

It was several seconds before she realised she ought to object to his masterful behaviour. 'Well, really, that's…' Her legs felt hollow and weak as, with shaking fingers, she smoothed down her hair.

One dark brow lifted. 'You have a problem with that?'

A tiny fractured sigh escaped her parted lips as she recalled with perfect clarity the way it had felt to run her hands covetously over the surface of his skin.

'No problem,' she whispered, mentally teasing her fingers into the dark fuzz of silky hair on his chest.

Resisting the abrupt and almost overwhelming urge to rip off his shirt and expose that golden expanse of hard flesh beaded her upper lip with sweat. She felt dizzy.

'What are you thinking about?'

The truth sprang to her lips. 'Touching you.'

His bronzed features clenched. 'I like your hands on me. I like you touching me.'

Her insides melted as a shard of sexual energy blasted through her feeble defences. 'And I *love* touching you,' she admitted in a small breathless whisper.

Her heart was thudding so loud that she could hardly hear her own voice. 'But, Luca, I think it isn't really a good idea…under the circumstances.'

'To hell with the circumstances!'

'Easy for you to say.'

'No, actually, it isn't.' His ironic laugh held a bewildering degree of bitterness. 'Not easy at all. Open the door, Alice.' He planted his hands palm-flat on the wall either side of her shoulders.

Alice instantly lost the ability to think or even breathe. His fingers slid into her hair, loosening the clip that held it in a casual twist on her head; it fell down into a silky sheet around her shoulders. He cupped her chin in his hand and tilted her head up to him.

'You want me. Say it!' he demanded fiercely.

Alice shuddered and closed her eyes as surrender flooded through her body. 'I want you, Luca.'

CHAPTER TWELVE

ALICE placed the item on the neatly packed suitcase and sat down on the bed. She felt her small self-congratulatory smile was well deserved; she hated packing with a vengeance and couldn't understand people who happily lived out of a suitcase. It was definitely not the lifestyle for her.

Of course the travelling she got to do with work had seemed very glamorous at first to a girl who had never been on a plane until she was twenty. She had not been a cool teenager, and family holidays when she was young had been a seaside boarding house in Cornwall, before it was a trendy destination. She had shared a room with her sister and slept in a bottom bunk that wouldn't have accommodated a plump Cornish kipper let alone a growing girl!

She had recollections of lots of rain, compulsory board games in the evening, and a fair number of family squabbles. All memories she treasured. Basically she was a girl who needed roots and that was where she was headed for a fortnight's holiday in the bosom of her family to recharge her depleted batteries.

Her expression softened as she thought of her home. Her father had been retired for several years. Not as spry as he once had been and with no son or daughter who wanted to work the land, he had sold all but a few of his acres off to a neighbour several years earlier. However, the half-timbered farmhouse with its odd-shaped rooms, low ceilings and passages that led nowhere was still the place where the brood returned and Alice was no exception.

This time was different. The tug of her roots was still as strong as ever, but she knew that the moment she walked through the door her mother would *know*. There was no *maybe* involved. It was spooky, but her mother always knew about these things. Her husband laughingly claimed she would have been called a witch in an earlier century.

Alice wasn't sure she wanted her feelings for Luca to be poked and prodded even by her liberal-minded mum. How was she going to admit that she had fallen in love with someone who had forgotten she even existed?

Her mother had been the only one to express concern when she and Mark had announced their engagement.

'I know you both like the same films and support the same football team. I'm sure you're as compatible as hell, sweetheart, but is he the love of your life?' she asked Alice on the evening of her engagement party. 'Are you sure you're not marrying because everyone expects you to?'

Alice was hurt by the question. 'Don't you like Mark, Mum?' she asked.

'Of course I like him. That's not the question; he's a very likeable boy. Do you love him? That's the only question that counts.'

'Of course I do,' she responded and at the time she believed it, but now Alice knew there was more than one way to love a man. Comparing what she had felt for her husband with what she felt for Luca was like comparing a gentle summer breeze to a full-scale hurricane warning.

It was a warning she ought to have heeded!

Though Mum ought to approve, Alice thought. I did what she always told me I ought to—I followed my instincts!

And where did it get me?

It had been three whole days since their last passionate encounter, and it had meant so much to Luca he hadn't even picked up a phone to call her since. She knew because she'd been waiting for it to ring…her heart racing every time she leapt to answer it and her spirits plummeting when she didn't hear his voice.

Her expression hardened as she gazed bleakly into the distance. Luca's method of giving the brush-off was brutal but efficient and he didn't even have to do anything, just make himself unavailable. Alice had got the message loud and clear. She just wished she had got it before she had rung his office number and got through to a nervous-sounding temp.

Alice could understand why she sounded nervous; she didn't see Luca as being an easy man to work for. Perfectionists rarely were, in her experience.

'Miss Trevelyan…sorry, you're…bear with me, I'd better check. Hold on a sec.'

Alice heard a few rustles and bangs and realised the harassed temp had obviously left the receiver lying on her desk.

'There's an Alice Trevelyan on the line asking for you?'

Alice winced and held the phone a little way from her ear as the voice continued loudly. 'Shall I put her through?'

Alice was looking at the tickets in her hand, wondering what she'd do if Luca hated the ballet, when down the line she heard a door slam.

'This is the intercom…next time use it.'

Alice winced in sympathy at the cutting derision in Luca's exasperated voice.

Despite that, I could listen to his voice all day, she found herself thinking.

'Sorry, sir, I just…sorry. Shall I put Miss Trevelyan through?'

'No.'

The contemplative smile that lifted the corners of Alice's wide mouth snuffed out. She lifted her hand to her mouth and a chill spread through her body as every last vestige of colour leeched from her face.

'What shall I say?'

'Use your imagination, but I don't want to speak to her. Is that clear?'

'Yes, absolutely, you don't want to speak to Miss Trevelyan.'

Alice replaced the phone down on the cradle with exaggerated care; she was shaking with hurt bewilderment. With stricken eyes she stared at the silent phone.

Oh, yes, she had got the message all right.

Was he more interested in the chase than anything that might follow? It certainly looked that way and she had made a terrible mistake. She had believed that what had passed between them was more than great sex. She had been misguided enough to imagine what they had shared was special...she was special.

What was she feeling? Humiliation, pain, anger and regret? Did she regret what had happened? Would she actually play it differently if the choice were offered her now?

Would she *not* have that memory?

God, why am I doing this? she wondered. The man didn't even have the decency to dump me and I'm obsessing about him. Would it have been so hard for him to issue some face-saving platitude like 'I think you're a lovely girl and we've had a great time but this isn't going to work out' in person?

'I'm doing it again!' she cried out loud. 'Say this after me, Alice...I will not think about Luca O'Hagan. He is not worth wasting one second of one minute on.' She gave a decisive nod and picked up the control for the TV while she finished packing.

She was flicking between a cartoon channel and a documentary on volcanoes when there was a knock on the door. Tucking a stray strand of hair behind her ear, she pulled it open with one hand while still looking at the screen.

'Hello, Alice.'

The voice made her freeze. She dropped the remote and poked her head around the door. Her eyes widened to their fullest extent. 'Oh, God, no!' she gasped and ducked back inside.

Standing with her back to the wall, she pressed her hand to her head and released a silent groan.

I can't believe I did that!

I could have spent a week figuring out how to look a total idiot and not come up with something that good. She turned her face to the wall and rested her forehead against the neutrally painted surface. A slick one-liner, that's what I need. A glib phrase that will leave me with a crumb of self-respect.

'Go away!' she heard herself growl.

That wasn't the line.

'You were very much nicer to me the last time we met.'

She could hear the nasty tone in his voice. Anger made her feel courageous. Chin up, eyes blazing with anger, she stepped into the doorway. 'I must have been drinking,' she choked. Even though she knew it had meant nothing to him, the memory of their lovemaking was precious to Alice. That he could use it to mock her hurt her beyond measure.

'Next you'll be saying you didn't know what you were doing.'

'I knew what I was doing,' she agreed quietly. 'The same way I know I'm not going to do it ever again.'

She definitely hadn't known what she was doing when she made the mistake of looking directly into his eyes. Normally expressive, his blue eyes were flat like a bottomless lake, nothing in them but her own reflection. It took all of her not inconsiderable will-power to break the hypnotic pull of those impenetrable orbs.

'So you no longer want me?' His expressive brows quirked. 'You want us to have a platonic relationship?'

Breathing hard, she gazed at the shiny surface of his leather boots while she tried to collect her thoughts. As her glance climbed over his long legs and muscular thighs clad in faded denim and moved upwards to his taut midriff and broad chest, so did her heart beat until it was pounding so hard she felt light-headed and breathless.

'I don't want us to have any sort of relationship.'

His nostrils flared. 'You think you can dismiss me the way you do your one-night stands?'

'One-night stands!' she gasped.

He looked into her wide eyes filled with bewilderment and stifled the irrational urge to comfort her. 'Don't look like that.' Voice harsh, he lowered his eyes. 'Sex is sex, you said.'

'I did no such thing…oh…!' Alice broke off, her eyes widening as her face flushed with colour. She did have the distinct recollection of saying something not dissimilar. 'I didn't mean—'

Luca cut her off with an imperative gesture. 'I know you probably don't think about it in those terms,' he conceded heavily. 'I suppose in your own peculiar way you think you're staying faithful to the memory of your dead husband. But the bottom line is avoiding involvement is—'

'Something you'd know all about,' she supplied, white with fury. 'A lecture on morals from you of all people. Do me a favour!'

There was a short static silence. Their eyes locked. 'That's exactly what I intend to do,' he said, before barging past her into the room.

Alice stayed where she was, her hand curled over the door handle; she wasn't too proud to run away. In fact the longer she considered the option, the more appealing it seemed. She kept her wary eyes trained on him as he sauntered across the room.

The navy cashmere sweater he wore had designer written all over it. It made his eyes look even more startlingly blue than usual…if that were possible! He had casually pushed the sleeves up, revealing the light sprinkling of dark hair on his sinewed forearms.

The stab of lust she experienced was so all-consuming that she was literally paralysed with longing. The paralysis was not just physical; she couldn't think…she couldn't breathe…

How long was I standing there eating him up with my eyes? The truth was she didn't have the faintest idea. It could have been half an hour or seconds but she sincerely hoped it was closer to the latter estimate!

Tiny muscles along her delicate but firm jaw quivered as she inhaled.

He ran a hand over his aggressive jaw, drawing Alice's attention to the dark designer stubble that covered the lower half of his face. Fairly predictably the almost piratical look it gave him was wildly attractive.

'It's a new look for you,' she said, simulating amusement. 'Very moody and if you're sporting it I'm sure it's all the latest fashion.'

His hand fell to his side. 'You think I'm a fashion victim?'

'I'm sure you couldn't give a damn what I think,' she returned with a carelessness she was a long way from feeling.

'I didn't come here to play word games.'

'Why did you come?'

So far her own efforts to figure this one out had not been productive. This could have something to do with the fact she was on some sort of intellectual hamster wheel. Her thoughts were stuck in a nightmare loop and nothing that was happening made any sense to her.

Luca, who was looking at the luggage neatly stacked on the bed, didn't appear to hear her question.

'You going somewhere?'

'Yes.'

His questioning glance didn't waver. 'Home,' she supplied reluctantly. 'I'm booked on the nine-thirty flight. So if you don't mind I need to finish—'

'It's lucky I got here in time, then, isn't it? Have you told your family?'

She gave a puzzled nod. 'I planned this holiday last year.'

'That's not what I was talking about and you know it,' he contended grimly.

'I don't know anything!'

Her heart-felt protest made him turn back towards her, and

the light from the east-facing window fell directly across his face. Alice's stomach tightened. Whatever else Luca was, she thought as her eyes moved over the strong, powerful contours of his amazing face, he was beautiful.

Swallowing, she lowered her pain-filled gaze.

'Look, Luca, I can see how you might think my door and my bed is always open to you when your plans for the evening have fallen through.' She caught her lower lip between her teeth, hating the embittered note in her voice. 'We had a nice time, but trying to recreate a mood is, in my experience, all too frequently disappointing. Let's keep the memory.' An inspired response if I say so myself.

She was too miserable to take any pleasure from his confounded, furious expression.

'We managed to recreate the *mood* pretty successfully once. Or were you *disappointed*?'

Her teeth clenched. She would have loved to wipe that smug, self-satisfied expression from his face. 'You know I wasn't,' she admitted with painful honesty. 'But please don't run away with the idea you could *recreate* anything again with me.'

'Actually I didn't come here to recreate any mood.'

The anger in his face extinguished any unrealistic hopes she had been nursing that this scene was going to follow the same format as one of her romantic fantasies. The ones that ended up with him telling her he had realised she was the only woman for him.

She gave a small derisive sniff. 'Well, why don't you tell me why you came before I lose the will to live?'

'I said I *didn't*, not that I *couldn't*. We both know that I could.'

'God knows what I ever saw in you!' she yelled.

'My incredible modesty?' There was a redeeming hint of self-mockery in his arrogant suggestion. 'Or my giving nature?'

'Will you take your giving nature and go away? I'm trying very hard to be polite. I can't guarantee I'll stay polite,' she warned him darkly. 'You know, I think I'd quite enjoy a scene right now.'

He folded his arms across his chest and trained his glittering gaze on her angry face. Alice's rigid spine felt as though it would snap. 'Bring it on, girl. Conflict is mother's milk to me—my mother's Latin and my father's Irish. Communication is always loud and dramatic in our house...especially loud.'

'That sounds tiring,' she said, almost as distracted by the picture his words conjured as she was by trying not to breathe in the musky scent of the fragrance he used. 'I hate arguments. I didn't know your parents' marriage wasn't...'

'Solid?' he suggested, looking amused. 'It remains a beacon of hope in these days of disposable marriages. Some people thrive on conflict, but, yes, I agree it's not relaxing. But Dad's heart attack means they have calmed things down. These days they count to ten before they let rip with the four-letter words. But I didn't come here,' he said grimly, 'to talk about my parents.'

'For heaven's sake, you keep saying what you didn't come for! Why did you come here?'

'I'm getting to that...' he promised, dragging a hand through his hair. A spasm of irritation crossed his face. 'Will you come in here and close that damned door? Maybe you don't mind sharing your business with the world but I do.'

Alice's expression hardened at his brusque demand. If it hadn't been for the maid outside her room who had dusted the same spot six times she would have ignored him.

'Door closed.' She flashed him an insincere smile. 'Now say your piece...not that I can imagine anything you say will be of interest to me,' she observed.

Luca studied the floor, tracing a pattern with the toe of his shiny boot in the deep pile of the carpet. Exhaling deeply, he lifted his eyes. 'I've been thinking about this situation and I think it would be the best solution all around if we got married.'

Not interested? Oh, boy, when I'm wrong about something I'm *really* wrong!

The seconds ticked away while she stared at him in open-mouthed disbelief.

'You think that we should get married?' The fact Alice's voice held no emotion was a reasonably fair reflection of her feelings; she was simply too numb to feel anything.

Luca's mouth twisted impatiently as he gave a curt nod. 'Isn't that what I just said?'

The knife-edged steely stare that accompanied this testy reply had very little of the desperate lover and a hell of a lot of anger. Even if you allowed for the fact Luca might not be a man particularly in touch with his feminine side, his attitude was not that generally expected of a man proposing.

Alice braced her shoulders against the wall as a wave of desolation of breathtaking intensity washed over her. She reached out blindly and her hand closed over the back of a chair; she was grateful for the support.

'Is this some sort of joke?' For one brief, blissful moment she had thought his proposal was for real...that he was here to tell her that he loved her. How much of a fool does that make me? she asked herself. 'Or have you discovered you can't live without me?'

Ironically that was exactly what he had discovered. In fact after three days he had accepted that bringing up another man's child as his own was preferable to living without this woman. His nostrils flared as his eyes ran over the ripe curves of her body. The fact he had no control whatever over the primitive response of his own body brought an angry rasp to his voice.

'Hardly...'

'So, the living without me you can manage, but you want to marry me? Curiouser and curiouser...' In stark contrast to her amused tone Alice felt physically sick when she realised how close she had come to making a total idiot of herself.

She cringed when she imagined what Luca's reaction would have been if she had followed her first impetuous instincts and flung herself at him. Now that would have been embarrassing!

'This is so unexpected,' sheer nerves made her flippantly trill.

'I'm sure some people appreciate your infantile sense of humour, but I am not one of them.'

'In that case I definitely can't marry you. The man I marry will definitely have to laugh at my jokes.'

'Shall we be serious?'

'Not easy…'

'This is not a decision I make lightly. Marrying me would solve a lot of problems for you.'

'You being the matrimonial catch of the century?' she suggested.

'You being an unmarried mother.'

Alice eyes widened. *Mother!* Slowly she shook her head. She held up her hand and hoarsely protested, 'Back up there! You think I'm pregnant?' I'd have to eat an awful lot of cheese to get a nightmare this surreal.

'We could waste time pretending, but this seems pointless. I'm assuming the father doesn't want to know? Have you told him or anyone else? I know you haven't told Roman. Presumably you'd planned to tell your family face to face?' He looked at her expectantly.

Alice stared at him, unable to believe what she was hearing. 'You told Roman I'm pregnant?' she said blankly.

'Of course I didn't tell him,' Luca responded with an irritated frown. 'I just asked a few leading questions and it was obvious he didn't have a clue, but he did confirm that you're not in a relationship.' For the first time Luca's rigid poise showed signs of cracking. 'It was also clear from what he said that you do have plenty of offers.'

A choking sound escaped Alice's white lips. 'How dare you discuss me with your brother?'

'Now listen, this is important. Alice, are you paying attention?' he rapped.

Alice's bloodless lips parted, then closed again. She shook her head. 'Oh, you have my full attention,' she promised hollowly.

Luca, his expression grave, nodded and ran a hand over the dark growth that covered his lean cheek. 'Does anyone but me know that you're pregnant?'

She shook her head. 'Not a soul,' she told him truthfully.

Some of the tension went out of his shoulders as he began to pace the room. 'Right, and it can stay that way.' He flashed her a look as if he expected her to protest. When she didn't he inclined his head. 'I'm glad you're going to be sensible about this.'

'You are?'

'As far as the world is concerned this baby is mine.'

'Why would you want people to think that?'

'I suppose you know my father had a heart attack some years ago?' Alice nodded. 'And it's important he doesn't subject himself to undue stress?'

'I really don't see what this has to do with—'

'My father is an old-fashioned man in many ways, deeply religious and proud of the family name,' Luca revealed gravely.

Alice, who had gathered as much from things that Roman had let drop, nodded cautiously.

'He has this thing, bordering on obsession actually, about continuing the line…the pride of the family name and all that. You probably know that Roman had a near miss marriage-wise. That broke Da's heart,' he admitted. 'He's been getting really worked up about the unmarried-sons-no-grandchild situation lately. So much so that Ma is seriously concerned about his health.'

Luca saw no need to explain that Natalia's concern hadn't prevented her expressing her opinion with fiery Latin bluntness that, the more her husband nagged, the less likely it became that she would ever have a grandchild because *his* sons were just as pigheaded and stubborn as their father.

'I'm sorry about your father, but I—'

Luca's expression became grave. 'His last check-up was not what anyone was expecting.' The consultant had been so amazed that he had taken his patient off almost all his medication.

'That's sad, but—'

'The fact is one of us has to get married.' Alice's eyes widened at this drastic solution. 'With his history, Roman is out; that leaves me.'

'You plan to get married to—'

'If you could make some small sacrifice that would save your father's life, wouldn't you make it?'

'Of course I would but—'

'Then why shouldn't I do the same?' he asked. 'I need a wife and baby, you are having a baby that needs a father. You must see the advantages of marrying me. Obviously we will draw up a pre-nup that protects your interests.'

'What more could I want?'

'You mean sex.'

'No, I damned well don't!' she rebutted furiously. 'Sex is all you ever think about.'

'I think that's what people in the trade call transference.'

'My God, get over yourself!' she advised with a caustic laugh. 'The person that is in urgent need of psychiatric care around here isn't me. I'm very sorry your father is ill, but your idea is totally crazy.'

'I'm assuming that mood swings and irrational behaviour are to be expected when you're pregnant. Let's calm down and deal in realities.'

'I'm perfectly calm!' she gritted through clenched teeth.

'It's tough bringing up a baby alone and my wife would lead a very comfortable life.'

'Pretty poor compensation for having to see you every day.'

'There will be no need for us to live in each other's pockets. There are many successful marriages where the partners lead separate lives.' His sensual lips curled. 'In fact they might actually be the most successful ones.'

Her hands clenched into fists as she listened to him outline what he obviously imagined were selling points of this proposed union…or should it be merger? she wondered bitterly.

'Gosh! When you put it *that* way how can I say no?' Her expression of brainless adoration morphed into one of hard-eyed anger.

'I really don't think you're in any position to cut off your nose to spite your face.'

'Thank you for the reminder.'

'There are not just your feelings to consider,' he reproached.

'Yes, but maybe I'm terminally selfish. Or maybe I don't like moral blackmail. You know, the longer I'm in your company, the more attractive being a single parent seems.' Suddenly Alice had had enough of this farce. 'You stupid man, there is no child!' She pressed her hands flat against her belly. 'I may look pregnant compared to those rakes you normally see naked, but I'm just fat and if I was having a baby I wouldn't lumber it with a father like you!'

Luca gave a derisive snort. 'For God's sake, woman, stop lying. I was standing outside the door when you rang for the test results.'

'Test results, but not *my* test results. You heard me ringing the clinic for my sister-in-law. The only thing I'm expecting is a niece or nephew. And for your information you're the only man I've slept with other than my husband and we actually waited until our wedding night. I'd like to say it was worth the wait, but we were both pretty clueless and it took us a couple of months to get the hang of things.' She stopped, appalled by what she had said.

Luca was staring at her, a hand pressed to the side of his head; he looked like a man who had just received a blow to the head. His eyes dropped to her middle. *'You're not pregnant?'*

'Finally…' she breathed.

'And you've not had any other lovers?'

'No.' She gave a bitter smile.

For a long moment he studied her with blank, stunned eyes. Then abruptly and with none of his usual natural grace he turned and walked to the window. The lines of his back screamed with tension.

When he turned back his face was wiped clean of emotion. 'It would seem that I made a mistake.'

'Not nearly as big a mistake as I made.' I fell in love with you, she nearly said.

His eyes slid from hers. 'Maybe we can retrieve something from this situation.'

'Like a lifelong friendship? I don't think so.'

'Then you wouldn't consider marrying me anyway?' Through the sweep of his lashes his brilliant eyes blazed.

She froze…marry him anyway? This had to be some twisted joke. He had loved her, left her, thought he could buy her, insulted her in every way possible and now this…! She drew a deep breath and fixed him with a look of loathing.

'Marry *you*? I think you're the most loathsome man I have ever met. I hate you! Marriage isn't about *sacrifice*, it's about *love* and I'm sure your father would agree with that if you asked him.'

Luca inclined his head. His face was like a slate wiped blank. 'He probably would,' he conceded. 'But you do things you might not otherwise consider when you love someone.'

'I appreciate you love your father, but if you need a wife I'm sure you won't have a problem finding someone other than me to say *I do*.' The day that advert appeared they'd be lined up around the block!

'I don't want anyone else.' The vehemence of his raw revelation made her blink. 'I want you, Alice.'

Alice closed her eyes. 'I don't want you,' she lied. He didn't love her.

'I slept with you when I thought you were carrying another man's child.' She heard his impassioned voice continue. 'I thought about not smelling your skin, you see, not feeling you quiver when I touch you, and I knew I had to have you one last time.' She heard a sound and imagined him raking his hand through his dark hair. 'I'm not proud of it. I spent too long successfully not touching you…' If he had touched her then she would have melted but he didn't. 'And now that I have I can't seem to stop. You're like a drug in my bloodstream.'

Alice opened her eyes to tell him she felt the same way and found she was alone.

CHAPTER THIRTEEN

ALICE couldn't let things stand that way. She had fully intended to contact Luca, and ask him if he had actually meant what he had said.

She rang New York as soon as she got home and discovered that nobody knew where Luca was; he had effectively vanished. Maybe he'd eloped, someone had laughingly suggested and Alice had felt sick…she'd been feeling sick a lot, actually. By the time he resurfaced, unmarried as it happened, she had discovered a complication.

Just a few months after she had told Luca that she wasn't pregnant, and she was. It was sometimes hard to think that the father of her child had a reputation for perception that bordered on the supernatural.

People might have noticed by now if the morning sickness hadn't been so bad, but rather than put on weight in the early weeks Alice had dropped over a stone. To her relief things were looking up and a glass of water no longer made her heave, so she knew it was only a matter of time before she started showing.

The fact she had to tell Luca soon was with her constantly. She didn't even have the excuse that she hadn't had the opportunity—she had. She still worked for Roman and Luca ran half the company; there had been any number of occasions when she had picked up the phone and heard his voice. In fact if anything she was forced to speak to him more often than usual, a circumstance that had made her seek out the bathroom on more than one occasion, not to throw up, but to cry her eyes out.

A couple of times she'd actually begun to tell him, but his curt response had always been so cold and impersonal that she hadn't been able to go through with it. It would have been like telling a total stranger you were carrying his child, especially when you had recently denied you were even pregnant. It sometimes seemed to Alice like another life when he had proposed and she had rejected him.

If Luca had ever been addicted to her it seemed to a miserable Alice that he had discovered the cure. She only wished she knew his secret.

Her normally super-observant boss hadn't picked up on any of the obvious signs, which wasn't like him. But Roman wasn't himself, due mostly, Alice suspected, to a new woman in his life.

She had known for sure that this Scarlet was something special when Roman had said he wouldn't be flying out to Ireland with her on Friday. He would, he'd explained, be on the ferry. When Alice had expressed her surprise at his choice he had explained, somewhat defensively, that Scarlet didn't like to fly.

'You'll like Scarlet,' he told her abruptly.

'I'm sure I will.'

'And Sam.'

'Her little boy…?'

'My son, actually.'

Having dropped the bombshell, he calmly walked into a meeting leaving her staring open-mouthed. Maybe this was why Luca was still unmarried? His father had the grandchild and, if she read the signs correctly, the marriage he had wanted too. That let Luca off the hook.

Alice ended up flying out to Ireland first class and alone. She was met at the airport by a chauffeur-driven limo and whisked away in style to the O'Hagan family estate. She had been here a couple of times before with Roman on working weekends but on those occasions she hadn't been carrying the O'Hagans' grandchild!

She was positively racked with guilt when Natalia went out of her way to make her feel welcome. She wondered if the welcome would have been quite so warm if she had known the truth. Mothers were notorious for siding with their sons and Natalia's pride when she spoke of hers was obvious.

'Make yourself at home, my dear. I know you like to walk and apparently this dry spell is set to last into next week. We're not expecting Roman until later. We're very excited,' she confided, confirming Alice's suspicion that there was a celebratory mood in the air.

Deciding to take her hostess's advice, she put on some walking shoes and a jacket intending to take a walk. She was actually opening the front door when the phone started ringing. Nobody appeared and it stopped, but almost immediately started up again.

Alice picked it up and before she had a chance to identify herself the person on the other end began to speak.

'Da, is that you?'

Alice almost dropped the phone. She stood there staring at the instrument in her hand for a long moment, shaking so hard that she almost dropped it. She swallowed past the dry constriction in her throat. 'No, it's me.' She closed her eyes and winced—he wouldn't know who *me* was.

He did.

'Alice…Alice, is that really you?' There was a crackling on the line and then his voice. 'Damn thing, it's cutting out and my flight…whatever you do don't…'

'Luca, I can't hear you. What are you saying?'

'Just don't do *anything* daft until I get there. I'll be there tonight. Alice, *cara*, promise me you won't do anything.'

'I promise,' she said without the faintest idea what she was promising.

Before the event Alice had been determined not to put a damper on things during dinner. So much for good intentions! She decided afterwards that it was that empty seat that had done it—made her lose it.

She had been wildly ambivalent about the news Luca was arriving, her mood swinging from wild hope to deep depression, but every time she looked at that empty seat where he ought to be sitting her eyes filled. It reached the point where she found it hard to breathe past the knot of misery lodged like a stone behind her breastbone.

After she had applied cold water to her tear-stained face following the short, frustratingly cryptic call she had received earlier from the airport, Alice had told his parents that Luca would be there for dinner.

She had been dreading their questions but beyond a, 'How lovely, all the family together,' Natalia, being extremely diplomatic, didn't pry further. Neither did her husband, though Alice suspected his silence was more to do with a discreet but well-aimed kick on the shins than diplomacy.

'I tried him earlier, but there was no answer on his mobile,' Roman said when Luca didn't show. 'I'll try him again.' He left the dinner table. When he returned he was shaking his head. 'Still no luck.'

'Well, there's no point waiting for him,' Finn O'Hagan, who had displayed none of the signs of infirmity Alice had been anticipating, said. 'I don't know what's got into him. Last night he cut me off right in the middle of a conversation. Cut me dead!' he added, shaking his head incredulously. 'If he's not got the manners to inform us he'll be late, he doesn't deserve the lovely meal your mother's organised.'

Natalia smiled her charming smile. 'But don't panic. When Finn says *organise* he doesn't mean I actually touched the food. I organised by nodding when Cook told me what she was making. Experience has taught me that if I do anything else she throws an artistic hissy fit and resigns.'

There was a ripple of amusement across the table.

'Mother is not renowned for her culinary skills,' Roman explained to the two young female guests. 'It takes dedication to burn water the way she does.'

As Alice stared at their laughing faces with disbelief, the distracting buzzing in her head got louder. Why was she the only one taking this seriously? The tight feeling in her chest continued to expand until she couldn't restrain herself any longer.

'Isn't anyone worried about where Luca is?' Pent-up anxiety made her voice loud and accusing. As a bottle stood poised above her wineglass she covered it with her hand and shook her head.

All eyes turned to her in response to her question.

'Knowing Luca, he could be anywhere,' his brother joked.

'He'll turn up,' his father predicted. Then added with a chuckle, 'The young devil always does, like the proverbial bad penny.'

This display of parental callousness fed the flames of Alice's growing anger.

'Oh, Cook will put aside some food for him, my dear,' Natalia said, stretching across the table to place a pat on Alice's hand.

Alice looked at the beautifully manicured hand covering her own and blinked. She couldn't believe what she was hearing. Hadn't it occurred to *any* of them that Luca could be in trouble?

'But he said he'd be here,' she reminded them, forcing a quick tight smile.

'Perhaps you misunderstood,' Roman suggested.

Scarlet, seated beside him, nodded. 'That's easily done,' she agreed.

'Maybe he meant tomorrow?' Roman ventured.

Their inability to appreciate the urgency of the situation

made Alice want to scream. 'Or maybe he didn't ring at all. That's probably what you're all thinking,' she accused wildly.

Somewhere in the dark, dim recesses of her consciousness she knew she had already said too much, she knew she was making a total idiot of herself, but she couldn't stem the flow.

'But he did ring,' she choked. 'And he said he'd be here tonight.'

'Maybe he just changed his mind,' Roman suggested tentatively.

Alice shook her head positively. 'Luca doesn't say things he doesn't mean.' She scanned the faces around the table and appealed, 'Hasn't it occurred to anyone that he may have had an accident?'

The colour drained from her overheated face as she envisaged Luca's lifeless body lying in an overturned car or worse, almost, he might be hurt and need her and she wasn't there!

'We should call the police!' She pressed her hand to her mouth as acid rose in her throat.

'My dear girl…' Finn began. He subsided when his wife pressed a warning hand to his arm. Slowly she shook her head before murmuring something in her native tongue to her eldest born, who nodded back.

'And so we shall, my dear,' she soothed.

Alice heaved a sigh of relief.

'If we don't hear from him before, we'll call them directly in the morning.'

'But—!' Alice began heatedly.

Natalia held up her hand, her expression kind but firm. 'They won't do anything unless someone is missing for twenty-four hours, you know, and the chances are he'll walk through that door any moment now.'

Alice bit her lip and, after a short pause, nodded. She looked around the table and realised that she had firmly established herself as the mad woman in their midst.

'I just thought…' She took a deep breath. 'I might have over-reacted,' she conceded.

'And then some,' Finn agreed with feeling before his wife silenced him with a frown, but not before a mortified flush had spread over Alice's pale skin.

It was Scarlet who smoothly came to her rescue.

She turned to her prospective father-in-law, who was not immune to the charm of her teasing smile. 'The trouble is, men lack imagination, and so they don't understand the curse of having an overactive one.' She forestalled the predictable male protest with an imperious wave of her hand. 'Whereas I can definitely empathise,' she admitted ruefully. 'Sam doesn't have a tummy ache, he has a burst appendix; he doesn't have a high temperature, he has meningitis. That's the way my mind works when it comes to Sam. I tell you, our doctor dreads hearing my voice and the practice nurses have coded me an NOPM… neurotic over-protective mum.'

Laughter and a general lessening of tension followed her droll disclosure. Alice mimed a thank-you across the table and Scarlet wrinkled her nose and gave a conspiratorial wink.

Alice smiled her way through the rest of dinner. She even managed to make a cheerful contribution when the after-dinner conversation turned to babies and weddings. Every time she replayed her spectacular loss of control she cringed and wished the floor would open up and swallow her, but she managed to hold it together until she said goodnight to Scarlet and Roman.

In fact, if she hadn't paused and turned back to make her last husky comment she would have got through the door with her smile intact.

'I'm so happy for you both,' she declared before bursting into tears.

'You can tell how happy she is, can't you, *cara mia*?' Roman observed, watching the tears stream down the cheeks of his cool and collected secretary.

'*Roman!*' Scarlet reproached, enfolding the sobbing woman in a comforting embrace.

'S…sorry,' Alice hiccuped as she wiped the moisture from her face and sniffed. 'I'm just…'

'No need to explain,' Scarlet interjected. 'I know *exactly* how you feel.'

'Is someone going to let me into the secret?' Roman enquired.

'Don't be so dense, Roman!' Scarlet chided impatiently.

'I'm assuming this has got something to do with my brother. If you've got any problems with him, come to me, Alice,' he suggested. 'I'll sort him out.'

'God, she's not that desperate!'

Alice had to look away…

Roman and Scarlet represented everything she wanted and would never have…*couldn't* have, unless Luca loved her—and, no easy way to say this, he didn't!

Self-pity, Alice, she reproached herself sternly, is not an attractive thing. Besides, she had other priorities now; like the child she was carrying. She had to tell Luca; on this subject at least there was no option.

She'd been through this in her head a million times before and a few barely intelligible words on the phone didn't change anything. She was pretty sure she knew how Luca would react when he knew about the baby. Luca called his father old-fashioned and proud of the family name, but he was just as proud; he was an O'Hagan.

He'd want to marry her for the sake of the baby.

There was no escaping the fact that Luca *was* the love of her life—and Luca would be resenting the fact he was tied to the mother of his child.

She sucked in a deep breath. 'No, I'm not that desperate,' she agreed quietly.

'Honestly, if you're worried about Luca, don't be,' Roman advised earnestly. 'He's got more lives than a cat,' he reflected. 'And he has a *very* well-developed sense of survival.'

She nodded. 'I'm sure you're right,' she agreed, on the outside, at least, calm.

'If you need me, you know where I am.' Scarlet, her pretty face a study of concern, caught Alice's arm.

Alice reminded herself that it had always been a long shot that anyone was going to swallow her show of disinterest close on the heels of her hysterical breakdown.

'I know,' she agreed, doubting that Roman would appreciate it if she took Scarlet up on the offer.

A glance at the grandfather clock ticking away in the hallway revealed it was still relatively early. The lure of another sleepless night and an intensive study of the wallpaper—no matter how tasteful—held a limited attraction for Alice. She responded to the plaintive cry of a sleek cat who had escaped from the kitchen and unbolted the grand front door.

The moggy vanished without a backward glance into the night and Alice stood there inhaling the sweet night air redolent of night-scented stock that someone had filled the tubs outside the door with.

Why not? she thought.

Feeling rather like a schoolgirl daringly ignoring a curfew, she pulled a jacket casually slung over the back of a chair in the hallway over her shoulders and went outdoors.

As she stepped outside the heavy door swung closed behind her with a decisive clunk. She shrugged; it wasn't as if she were locked out in the literal sense. Nobody here seemed to feel the necessity to lock anything. She could quite easily let herself in the side kitchen door after she had had a walk in the moonlight.

The night was simply magical…no street lights, just a moon and the smell of green growing things. Alice felt her mood lift.

The moment she stepped on the neatly trimmed lawn her high heels sank into the soft ground. After stumbling her way a couple of hundred yards, she slipped the shoes off and stuffed them in the jacket pockets.

Back to nature, she thought as she enjoyed the squidgy feel of the wet grass. Experimentally she wriggled her toes and discovered it was not actually unpleasant. An owl hooted eerily in the distance as she turned her face to the warm soft breeze that sprang up. Lost in thought, she walked until the lights from the house were a distant twinkle.

She reached a slight rise ahead as the parkland became woodland proper, and she stopped to catch her breath, realising for the first time how far she'd gone from the neatly manicured lawns. She began to wonder if she had maybe had enough of nature for one night. Maybe she ought to make her way back now?

Just as she was reflecting how easy it would be to imagine yourself the only person in the world out here a cloud drifted across the silver face of the full moon. It almost immediately lifted. Alice had lived in the City so long she had almost forgotten that dark in the country was not the same thing as dark in the town! Not by a long chalk!

Standing there, she rediscovered that the countryside at night was not actually quiet. If you listened as she was it was filled with sounds—soft, sinister rustling sounds, sounds made by things she couldn't see.

Now that she thought about it, she wasn't sure she wanted to see them. Come to think of it, what was she doing in the wilds of Ireland, alone, in the middle of the night?

It seemed a good idea at the time. That was probably what all the victims of mad knife-wielding psychopaths said, or *would* have if they hadn't been dead. She brushed aside her morbid fancies.

'A torch would be good!' She spoke out loud to steady her nerves. They stayed steady until the moon ducked once more behind a cloud at the same moment her hair snagged on a low branch.

Alice lost it. She let out a high-pitched scream and began running barefoot. By the time exhaustion made her stop she had lost her bearings totally.

Don't panic. What's the worst that can happen? *Excluding psychopaths!* She forced herself to think logically. She could get blisters, scratches and scare the odd sheep. It was a warm night so she wasn't going to get hypothermia. Gradually her racing heartbeat slowed.

Tomorrow she would laugh about this.

Despite her determinedly upbeat attitude tomorrow seemed an awful long way away.

She slid the shoes back on her dirty feet and cautiously now continued through the trees heading towards high ground, calculating that from that vantage point she might be able to see where she was.

Despite her efforts to spot landmarks around her, nothing around looked familiar. If I'd been a girl-guide this would have been a different story. Talk about wisdom in retrospect, she thought. The only survival tips she seemed to have picked up involved digging a hole in the snow and wrapping yourself in clingfilm…or was that tinfoil? Well, as she had neither, or for that matter snow, it wasn't terribly helpful.

'A trail of breadcrumbs is what I need,' she muttered as she gingerly picked her way around a bramble bush. Emerging unscathed the other side, she felt quite pleased until without warning she collided with a large warm body. A warm body that had hands, ones that grabbed her.

Instinct took over and she immediately tried to pull free, struggling frantically against her captor, whose grip lessened momentarily when she released a scream an Irish banshee would have been proud of.

During the short, frantic struggle that followed several of her wild blows and kicks found their target and she had the satisfaction of hearing her assailant grunt in pain more than once.

'I know karate,' she warned. 'I don't want to have to hurt you.'

'Congratulations, you're hiding your reluctance really well so far. Alice, *Madre di Dios*, will you calm down? I'm not going to hurt you.'

CHAPTER FOURTEEN

ALICE froze... She would have recognised that voice amongst a thousand others. In a split second she tumbled headlong from extreme terror and misery into total bliss!

'Luca?'

'Were you expecting someone else?'

The relief that flooded through her was profound as she collapsed weakly against him. He felt solid and deliciously real. Too real to be a dream.

'I can't believe...'

For a moment she saw his dark lean face, dappled by moonlight that shone through the leafy canopy overhead, before his mouth came crashing down. With a soft, muffled cry against his lips, she wound her arms around his neck; resistance didn't even enter her head.

There were tears running down her cheeks when he eventually lifted his head. He blotted them gently with the back of his hand.

'Believe now?' he said, breathing against her cheek.

She might have interpreted his tone as complacent if she hadn't been in a position to know that he was shaking, racking his greyhound-lean frame with fine tremors.

She sighed and cupped her hand around the side of his face. 'That was quite a hello.'

He turned his face into her hand and kissed the centre of her palm, sending a delicious shiver all the way to her bare toes. 'I'm known for my hellos.'

'So that was nothing special?'

His fingers tightened around the delicate bones of her wrist. 'Very special. I've been thinking about it for a long time. I wasn't sure about how welcome I'd be. But you seemed to be moderately glad to see me?' Luca's attempts to read her expression were frustrated by the shadow that lay over her face.

A plea for reassurance from Luca?

'Moderately glad, yes,' she agreed with overdue caution. 'How did you know I was here?'

'I didn't know, at least not that it was you, but I heard you from half a mile away. I thought you were a particularly noisy poacher.'

'I'm not a poacher.'

'That's good. You have no aptitude for it.'

'I was thinking about you,' she murmured, pressing her face into his chest. The feeling of intense relief was mingled with an overpowering sense of coming home. 'And you came,' she sighed softly. Nothing had ever sounded as good to her as the thud of his slow, steady heartbeat.

Luca held her as though he'd never let her go.

For several minutes she stood there as he stroked her hair, letting the mellifluous stream of passionate Italian that spilled from him wash over her.

When she finally lifted her head she saw that he was looking strained; his lean face in the moonlight was all stern, strong angles and fascinating shadows. Her breath caught in her throat... *Oh, my God, but he's beautiful!*

'You're really here?' She sighed happily.

'We'd already established that, *cara*. If we carry on covering old ground we could be here all night.'

'I just still don't understand how or why...' She looked around the leafy glade. 'Where is here?'

'You don't know?'

'I went for a walk; I got lost.'

'You thought that going for a walk in the middle of the night was a good idea? What the hell were they thinking of,' he snapped, 'letting you go out? They should have found you by now.'

'Nobody's looking. I didn't ask permission, Luca, and I doubt if anyone even knows I'm not in bed.'

'So you could have fallen and broken your leg and nobody would have been any the wiser.' She could hear the anger in his voice as he slid a finger inside the lapel of the borrowed jacket. She shivered as his fingertip slid along her collar-bone.

'I thought the fresh air would make me sleep. I lost a shoe,' she discovered. 'They cost a fortune.'

'Be grateful that's the only thing you lost!' he retorted harshly. 'When I think—' He broke off and cursed softly when he saw the glint of tears on her cheeks.

'I was lost,' she revealed plaintively. 'And scared, so don't shout at me.' With a shiver she cast a scared look over her shoulder. 'Is it far back to the house?'

Without replying he took her hand and led her to the top of the small rise; below them was the house illuminated by strategically placed spotlights.

'I thought I was miles away!' she gasped. 'When all along—'

'All you had to do was follow your nose,' he interjected, looking amused. 'And a very beautiful nose it is too.' He kissed the pink tip of her nose.

'You can laugh, but you were lost too.' Actually Luca wasn't laughing, he was looking at her as if he was committing every detail of her face to memory. Her erratic pulse rate kicked up another notch.

'Me…?' His deep voice held a dry satirical lilt but he still didn't smile. 'I swerved to avoid a loose horse and ended up in a ditch.'

The breaths nagged painfully in her throat. Without realising it she grasped his shirt, dislodging in the process the jacket draped around her shoulders.

'Were you hurt?' Her eyes ran down the lean, taut lines of his body but she could see no obvious signs of injury.

He shook his head. 'Would you have cared?'

She didn't respond to his soft taunt; the rampant hunger in his eyes was less easy to ignore. 'You didn't ring. We waited to have dinner.'

'But not long?'

She conceded the point with a shrug.

'The old man doesn't like to eat late,' he said drily. 'I suppose he wasn't happy…?'

'Actually everyone was pretty happy.' Except me, she wanted to say, but didn't.

'So nobody missed me?'

'We managed to muddle through without you.'

'That's good.'

Alice gave a snort of exasperation and pulled out of his arms. 'Would you prefer I said that I was worried sick…that I had a *totally* terrible night? If you must know I made a total fool of myself.' She pushed her fingers in her hair and shook her head back and forth in weary disbelief. 'Your parents think I'm a lunatic.' She arched a brow. 'Does *that* make you any happier?'

'Looks like I missed quite a night. Are you hugging that tree?' he asked as she walked over to a large oak and laid her face tiredly against the bark.

It stops me hugging you.

'Don't worry, you didn't miss that much.' Besides my disintegration into a raving lunatic. 'You'll be able to catch up on the wedding arrangements; nobody is talking about much else.' In the darkness she couldn't see the colour leave his face.

'There isn't going to be a damned wedding.'

'W…what are you talking about? Of course there's going to be a wedding; everyone's so excited.'

'For God's sake, woman, you promised me you wouldn't do anything!' he groaned.

'And I haven't.'

'You call saying you'll marry my brother nothing? You're both insane if you think I'm going to let that happen. You can't settle for second-best. I know you think you'll never feel the way about anyone like you did your husband,' he admitted. 'And Roman's got this crazy idea he's never going to find love after being dumped. Dad's been getting to him lately, but believe me he's a lot tougher than he looks.'

'But…Luca…I'm…'

'I know I behaved like an idiot. I know I messed up big time when I proposed, but the idea of you bringing up a baby alone just…I just couldn't let that happen.'

'Why were you willing to bring up another man's child?'

'It wasn't an easy decision to make,' he admitted. 'But once I realised the important thing was that it was *your* child too, I knew what I had to do,' he explained simply. 'These last few weeks have been hell. You must have realised half those calls I put through to the office were just so that I could hear your voice.'

'They were?' she gasped, enchanted by this revelation. 'You sounded so cold and distant,' he accused.

She pressed her hand to his lips. 'Stop it, Luca, I'm not marrying Roman.'

'Damn right you're not,' he growled, kissing her finger.

'He's got engaged to Scarlet.'

'Scarlet?'

'You'll like her,' Alice promised. 'And Sam.'

'Who the hell is Sam?'

'Sam is Roman's son.'

'Dio mio,' he breathed in a shaken voice. 'I have missed a lot. I knew you were here, and when Da said on the phone that I was off the hook because according to Mum the chances were Roman was finally about to tie the knot…' He appealed to her. 'What was I supposed to think?'

'On past experience, something really stupid. Luca, darling, I'm only crazy about one of the O'Hagan brothers.'

'I got on the first flight I could,' he revealed in a harsh, driven voice. Alice stood there in the darkness, tears streaming down her face, *feeling* the pain she heard in his voice. 'When I reached London I rang…you answered and it seemed like my worst fears were confirmed. If only I'd had the guts to come out and tell you how I actually felt.' He stopped abruptly, his lean body stiffening.

'What did you just say?' he demanded in a raw voice. 'What did you call me?'

'*Darling*. Luca, you asked me to marry you once and I said no…'

'You said more than that, *cara*.' His hand moved to her cheek. 'You're still crying?'

'I didn't mean what I said. I was hurt and angry and I've regretted it so many times since,' she admitted.

'I deserved it,' he said. 'I suppose you realise by now that Da is in no danger of dropping dead if I don't get married. I was wrong.'

'You were a manipulative snake.'

He didn't offer any excuses. 'Listen, I *totally* accept that Mark was an important part of your life,' he told her urgently. 'But you have to move on…'

'I have moved on. Luca, will you marry me?'

The silence stretched until Alice, who had been serenely confident about what she was doing moments earlier, started to think she'd made a terrible mistake.

'What did you say?' His voice was barely recognisable.

'I said will you marry me, Luca?'

'Why?'

She closed her eyes, took a deep breath and stepped right off the cliff. 'Because,' she replied in a clear, confident voice, 'I love you. I love you more than I thought was possible.' The breath whooshed out of her lungs as he enfolded her in a satisfyingly hungry, rib-crushing embrace.

Luca kissed her until she forgot where she began and he ended. While it lasted the rest of the world ceased to exist for Alice.

'Is that a yes?' she asked shakily when they finally surfaced.

Luca ran a finger down her smooth cheek. 'What do you think?'

'I think I'd like to hear you say it.'

'Yes, of course yes, you idiot woman. And of course I love you, Alice, my first and last true love. Why else would I have done what I did tonight? I mean, what sane man would throw his phone over a hedge when the batteries run low and hike ten miles cross country?'

'Gracious,' she exclaimed. 'Is that what you did?'

'Damn right I did.'

'You could have got lost.'

'No. Roman and I know this place like the back of our hands. We used to camp out here—' he gestured towards the sinister-looking craggy peak silhouetted to the north '—and fish through the night on the lough.'

'I can understand your desire to recapture your youthful exploits as a wilderness man but—and I know I'm a tenderfoot, but wouldn't it have been easier to go to the nearest house and use the telephone?'

'Most probably, but you forget you're talking to a man in love here and all I could think about was getting to you.'

'And now you're here.' She couldn't stop smiling. 'Luca, there's something I haven't told you…'

'And what might that be?' he asked lovingly. 'Is something wrong?' he added, suddenly picking up on her tension.

'I don't think so and I hope you won't think so either. I didn't tell you before because—'

'If there was someone else while we were apart I'll understand. It's probably my fault,' he gritted. 'But I don't want to know any of the details.'

'Of course there was nobody else!' The cloud lifted from the moon and she saw the intense relief on his strong face. 'If you must know, I've spent the last few weeks with my head down the toilet.'

He shook his head. 'You've been ill…you are thin…'

'Not ill, Luca, having a baby, your baby.' She pressed her hand to the gentle swell low on her belly and smiled. 'Our baby. I really am pregnant this time.'

If she had had any doubts about his feelings, the look of sheer, incredulous joy and fierce pride that blazed across his face would have put them to rest.

'I knew you'd marry me because of the baby,' she explained quietly. 'I just wanted to know if you'd marry me for me, Luca.'

His electric-blue eyes darkened. 'I'd marry you in a heartbeat.' He took her face between his hands and pressed a long, lingering kiss to her lips. When he pulled back he sighed. 'I'm over the moon about the baby, Alice, but you're the centre of my universe and you always will be.'

Moved beyond words, she felt tears sting her eyelids.

'Hormones…?' he queried, touching his thumb to a solitary tear rolling down her cheek.

She shook her head. 'Happiness,' she corrected huskily.

With an instruction to, 'Hold on tight,' he suddenly scooped her up into his arms. 'Come on, let's go and tell everyone the news.'

'You can't carry me all the way back.'

'I can not only carry you all the way back, I can leap tall buildings.'

'My superhero,' she sighed, looping her arms about his neck. 'Luca, you're not really going to tell everyone now, are you?'

'Of course I am. I want everyone to know how lucky I am.'

'But, Luca, it's the middle of the night and they'll all be asleep.'

He looked unimpressed by this argument. 'Not after I wake them up, they won't be,' he observed with a complacent smile.

'I appreciate you want to shout it from the rooftops, but just for tonight can it be just you and me?'

'It's going to be you and me for the rest of our lives, Alice.'

His blue eyes were filled with so much love that she gasped. Alice suddenly saw the future…their golden future together stretching ahead of them. Could one person have this much happiness…?

'No, you're right,' she said with an impish grin. 'Let's wake up the house!'

And they did. The O'Hagans were proud and stubborn, but wow did they know how to party!

* * * * *

Silhouette Desire kicks off 2009 with
MAN OF THE MONTH, *a yearlong program
featuring incredible heroes by stellar authors.*

When navy SEAL Hunter Cabot returns home for some
much-needed R & R, he discovers he's a married man.
There's just one problem: he's never met his "bride."

*Enjoy this sneak peek at Maureen Child's
AN OFFICER AND A MILLIONAIRE.
Available January 2009 from Silhouette Desire.*

One

Hunter Cabot, Navy SEAL, had a healing bullet wound in his side, thirty days' leave and, apparently, a wife he'd never met.

On the drive into his hometown of Springville, California, he stopped for gas at Charlie Evans's service station. That's where the trouble started.

"Hunter! Man, it's good to see you! Margie didn't tell us you were coming home."

"Margie?" Hunter leaned back against the front fender of his black pickup truck and winced as his side gave a small twinge of pain. Silently then, he watched as the man he'd known since high school filled his tank.

Charlie grinned, shook his head and pumped gas. "Guess your wife was lookin' for a little 'alone' time with you, huh?"

"My—" Hunter couldn't even say the word. *Wife?* He didn't have a wife. "Look, Charlie..."

"Don't blame her, of course," his friend said with a wink as he finished up and put the gas cap back on. "You being gone all the time with the SEALs must be hard on the ol' love life."

He'd never had any complaints, Hunter thought, frowning at the man still talking a mile a minute. "What're you—"

"Bet Margie's anxious to see you. She told us all about that R and R trip you two took to Bali." Charlie's dark brown eyebrows lifted and wiggled.

"Charlie..."

"Hey, it's okay, you don't have to say a thing, man."

What the hell could he say? Hunter shook his head, paid for his gas and as he left, told himself Charlie was just losing it. Maybe the guy had been smelling gas fumes too long.

But as it turned out, it wasn't just Charlie. Stopped at a red light on Main Street, Hunter glanced out his window to smile at Mrs. Harker, his second-grade teacher who was now at least a hundred years old. In the middle of the crosswalk, the old lady stopped and shouted, "Hunter Cabot, you've got yourself a wonderful wife. I hope you appreciate her."

Scowling now, he only nodded at the old woman—the only teacher who'd ever scared the crap out of him. What the hell was going on here? Was everyone but him nuts?

His temper beginning to boil, he put up with a few more comments about his "wife" on the drive through town before finally pulling into the wide, circular drive leading to the Cabot mansion. Hunter didn't have a clue what was going on, but he planned to get to the bottom of it. Fast.

He grabbed his duffel bag, stalked into the house and paid no attention to the housekeeper, who ran at him, fluttering both hands. "Mr. Hunter!"

"Sorry, Sophie," he called out over his shoulder as he took the stairs two at a time. "Need a shower, then we'll talk."

He marched down the long, carpeted hallway to the rooms that were always kept ready for him. In his suite, Hunter tossed the duffel down and stopped dead. The shower in his bathroom was running. His *wife?*

Anger and curiosity boiled in his gut, creating a churning mass that had him moving forward without even thinking about it. He opened the bathroom door to a wall of steam and the sound of a woman singing—off-key. Margie, no doubt.

Well, if she was his wife...Hunter walked across the room, yanked the shower door open and stared in at a curvy, naked, temptingly wet woman.

She whirled to face him, slapping her arms across her naked body while she gave a short, terrified scream.

Hunter smiled. "Hi, honey. I'm home."

* * * * *

Be sure to look for
AN OFFICER AND A MILLIONAIRE
by USA TODAY *bestselling author Maureen Child.*
Available January 2009 from Silhouette Desire.

HARLEQUIN Presents

EXCLUSIVELY HIS

Back in his bed—and he's better than ever!

Whether you shared his bed for one night or five years, certain men are impossible to forget! He might be your ex, but when you're back in his bed, the passion is not just hot, it's scorching!

CLAIMED BY THE ROGUE BILLIONAIRE

by Trish Wylie

Available January 2009
Book #2794

Look for more Exclusively His novels from Harlequin Presents in 2009!

Demure but defiant…
Can three international playboys
tame their disobedient brides?

Lynne Graham

presents

Proud, masculine and passionate, these men are used
to having it all. In stories filled with drama, desire
and secrets of the past, find out how these arrogant
husbands capture their hearts.

THE GREEK TYCOON'S DISOBEDIENT BRIDE
Available December 2008, Book #2779

THE RUTHLESS MAGNATE'S VIRGIN MISTRESS
Available January 2009, Book #2787

THE SPANISH BILLIONAIRE'S PREGNANT WIFE
Available February 2009, Book #2795

HP12787

MISTRESS
TO A
MILLIONAIRE

She's his in the bedroom, but he can't buy her love...

Showered with diamonds,
draped in exquisite lingerie,
whisked around the world...
The ultimate fantasy becomes a reality
in
Sharon Kendrick's

BOUGHT FOR THE SICILIAN BILLIONAIRE'S BED

Available Janary 2009
Book #2789

Live the dream with more
Mistress to a Millionaire titles
by your favorite authors

Coming soon!

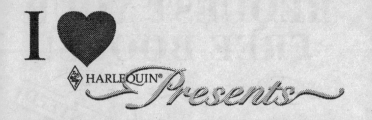

REQUEST YOUR FREE BOOKS!

HARLEQUIN *Presents* ®

2 FREE NOVELS
PLUS 2
FREE GIFTS!

PASSION GUARANTEED SEDUCTION

YES! Please send me 2 FREE Harlequin Presents® novels and my 2 FREE gifts (gifts are worth about $10). After receiving them, if I don't wish to receive any more books, I can return the shipping statement marked "cancel". If I don't cancel, I will receive 6 brand-new novels every month and be billed just $4.05 per book in the U.S. or $4.74 per book in Canada, plus 25¢ shipping and handling per book and applicable taxes, if any*. That's a savings of close to 15% off the cover price! I understand that accepting the 2 free books and gifts places me under no obligation to buy anything. I can always return a shipment and cancel at any time. Even if I never buy another book, the two free books and gifts are mine to keep forever.

106 HDN ERRW 306 HDN ERRL

Name _____ (PLEASE PRINT) _____

Address _____ Apt. # _____

City _____ State/Prov. _____ Zip/Postal Code _____

Signature (if under 18, a parent or guardian must sign)

Mail to the **Harlequin Reader Service:**
IN U.S.A.: P.O. Box 1867, Buffalo, NY 14240-1867
IN CANADA: P.O. Box 609, Fort Erie, Ontario L2A 5X3

Not valid to current subscribers of Harlequin Presents books.

Want to try two free books from another line?
Call 1-800-873-8635 or visit www.morefreebooks.com.

* Terms and prices subject to change without notice. N.Y. residents add applicable sales tax. Canadian residents will be charged applicable provincial taxes and GST. Offer not valid in Quebec. This offer is limited to one order per household. All orders subject to approval. Credit or debit balances in a customer's account(s) may be offset by any other outstanding balance owed by or to the customer. Please allow 4 to 6 weeks for delivery. Offer available while quantities last.

Your Privacy: Harlequin Books is committed to protecting your privacy. Our Privacy Policy is available online at www.eHarlequin.com or upon request from the Reader Service. From time to time we make our lists of customers available to reputable third parties who may have a product or service of interest to you. If you would prefer we not share your name and address, please check here. ☐

HP08R

Inside ROMANCE

Stay up-to-date on all your romance reading news!

The Inside Romance newsletter is a FREE quarterly newsletter highlighting our upcoming series releases and promotions!

Click on the <u>Inside Romance</u> link on the front page of **www.eHarlequin.com** or e-mail us at insideromance@harlequin.ca to sign up to receive your FREE newsletter today!

You can also subscribe by writing us at: HARLEQUIN BOOKS Attention: Customer Service Department P.O. Box 9057, Buffalo, NY 14269-9057

Please allow 4-6 weeks for delivery of the first issue by mail.

IRNBPA208

HIS VIRGIN MISTRESS

Bedded by command!

He's wealthy, commanding, with the self-assurance of a man who knows he has power. He's used to sophisticated, confident women who fit easily into his glamorous world.

She's an innocent virgin, inexperienced and awkward, yet to find a man worthy of her love.

Swept off her feet and into his bed, she'll be shown the most exquisite pleasure— and he'll demand she be his mistress!

Don't miss any of the fabulous stories this month in Presents EXTRA!

Available in January 2009

www.eHarlequin.com

HPE0109